all the best.

Julie Parker

SEND ME AN
Angel

Julie Parker

World Castle Publishing, LLC
Pensacola, Florida
Copyright © Julie Parker 2018
Hardback ISBN: 9781629899749
Paperback ISBN: 9781629899756
eBook ISBN: 9781629899763
First Edition World Castle Publishing, LLC, August 20, 2018
http://www.worldcastlepublishing.com

Cover: Karen Fuller
Editor: Maxine Bringenberg

Table of Contents

Chapter One

"Hi there, Ella. Ah, my son is selling chocolate bars for school. You know, the ones with nuts or something or other in them. I was wondering...."

Here it comes, Ella thought. Couldn't one blasted day go by without someone trying to squeeze her out of her dwindling funds? If it wasn't little Tommy selling chocolate, then it was a club selling raffle tickets. Or there was an invitation to a baby shower or a girl's night out. She was running out of excuses and catch-me-laters. It was a conspiracy, she just knew it.

"Sorry, Jim. I only have a fifty on me right now," she lied, silently praying he wouldn't say he could make change. The look on his face told her that he couldn't, and Ella smiled with relief. "Catch me another time, okay?"

"Ah, sure. Okay." Jim picked up his novel and headed toward the exit. Ella congratulated herself on another successful dodge. Now, if she could only think of something to say to the bank manager, she would have it made.

Leaning against the checkout counter of Caverly's library, she closed her eyes. It was close to noon and things should quiet down now that it was lunchtime. She needed time to think, but answering questions or helping people look for a certain book every few minutes was breaking her concentration. Jim had been the last person to check out, and as long as no one else entered, she might just be able to come up with an idea. She tried to imagine the perfect words that would make everything sound as though she had a brilliant plan in mind.

"Sleeping on the job again, are you?" Cate asked as she leaned against the counter beside Ella. "It's twelve o'clock, time to go for lunch," she prodded, as Ella looked at her with a blank stare.

"Oh, Cate." How could she forget that it was Friday and she had promised to join her for lunch? After putting her off so many times already, she was surprised that her friend hadn't stopped asking her altogether. "Rain check, okay?"

"Come on. Sarah can handle things until we get back."

"I'm sorry, really, but I've got a ton of errands to run."

"Can't you do them after work?"

"No. I promised Mrs. MacKenzie I'd pick up Calvin right after five o'clock. I can't be late, you know what she's like."

Cate sighed dramatically. "Oh, all right. But next week for sure, okay?"

"I promise," Ella said seriously, holding crossed fingers behind her back.

She ate a tuna fish sandwich while seated behind the wheel of her car ten minutes later. She had gone through the pretense of running off to do her errands, but in reality, she had just driven to the edge of town and pulled over onto a side street. The radio played softly so as not to disturb her thoughts.

The past week, since she'd gotten up the courage to call the bank, that had been all she could think about. To them, it was only an appointment for a small loan. But to her, it felt like the difference between life and death.

Two years ago, her husband and the father of her son, Calvin, had died. She had been surprised when she'd arrived home after work and found Brian and Ted, two of Caverly's police officers, sitting in front of her house. They had gently told her there'd been an accident and that Joe had been killed. Just like that, a few words, and her world had changed forever.

Ella had taken a leave of absence from her job at the library and stayed home for nearly six months to be with two-year-old Calvin, and to try to pull herself together. She had received a small amount of insurance money when Joe had died, but it hadn't taken long for it to disappear. Returning to work had been a necessity. Her financial situation had become desperate, and she needed the income from her job. Still, as it was, she made barely enough money to pay the mortgage, utilities, and basic necessities for Calvin and herself. Getting by day to day was a struggle.

A small loan from the bank, she felt, would temporarily solve some of her money woes. Although, getting it could prove to be difficult considering she had been late the past two months on her mortgage payments. Convincing the bank that she could repay the loan would be the problem, because they knew she didn't have Joe's income to rely on anymore.

At five o'clock, the time had come to face the music. The

appointment at the bank was at five-fifteen. Her destination was across town, and she hoped Cate or Sarah wouldn't by chance happen to drive by and see her car sitting at the bank when she'd told them she'd be picking up her son.

She jumped into her 2002 Neon and waited for what felt like forever for the driver's window to slowly slide down, letting the July heat escape. Once again she regretted her haste in trading in her 2012 Escape, but the extra five thousand dollars it had given her had come in handy.

Reaching the bank at precisely ten after five, Ella rushed inside and grabbed a seat outside the manager's office. He was on the telephone, but he had seen her come in and gestured for her to wait. She felt as though she were no longer twenty-six, but eight years old, sitting outside the principal's office.

"Ella? Come on in."

Ella entered the office and took a seat before Mr. Bentley's desk. He had her application sitting before him and he picked it up, appearing to give it considerable thought. But when he looked up at her and his smile turned patronizing, Ella knew that she was in trouble. His look reminded her of her uncle's before beginning one of his lectures.

In the end, the meeting went as she had expected. Mr. Bentley had been sympathetic to her situation, but he had ultimately denied her request. Her income, he explained, was not enough to cover her debts. Ella had pointed out that was the reason why she required the loan, but he argued she didn't have any way to repay the money. He had suggested a few ideas of how to cut costs, and even said that she should perhaps look into selling her house and renting something smaller. Filled with despair, Ella feared she might actually break down and beg the man for the money or start to weep hysterically. Instead, she had quickly thanked him for his advice and told him she would consider his suggestions. She'd gathered her purse and made a dash for the door with as much dignity as possible.

Her babysitter's house was located just outside of town, like Ella's. By the time she reached it, she had composed herself and even managed to smile kindly at Mrs. MacKenzie as she made her way up the front walk. The older woman had seen her drive up and stood waiting at the front door with Calvin. His little shoes were already on and his backpack hung from his shoulders. Ella wished she had the courage to ask the woman her secret. At her own home, it was always a fight every morning just to get him dressed. She knew Mrs. MacKenzie would gladly share her great wealth of knowledge. It was just that whenever she did so, she had a way of making Ella feel totally inadequate as a mother.

"Hello, my sweet baby," Ella said, lifting a struggling Calvin into her arms.

"Not a baby," he insisted, as he reluctantly allowed his mother to rain kisses on his cheeks.

Ella put him down to reach for the cash from her purse to pay Mrs. MacKenzie for the week. "How did it go today?" she asked as she counted out fives and tens, and to her embarrassment, the change she'd scrounged from the bottom of her purse.

Mrs. Mackenzie's manners were too proper to comment on the steadily growing handful of coins she was receiving. She did, however, lift an eyebrow slightly. "He was an angel as always, dear."

9

Ella thanked her and said she'd see her on Monday, then loaded Calvin into his car seat. She made her way through town, driving mechanically as she listened to her son's chatter. His little voice was sweet and soothing to her frayed nerves. Hearing him go on about his adventurous day brought home to her the importance of his well-being. He was what her life was all about now.

She pulled into the driveway of her home, a cozy three-bedroom side split, painted white with forest green shutters. As soon as she lifted Calvin down from his seat he ran up and waited by the front door while she grabbed his backpack. Once inside, he kicked off his shoes before hurrying off to his bedroom to play. Ella leaned down to set his shoes onto the mat.

As she stood by the closet she could hear the answering machine click on in the living room, and realized she must have just missed hearing the phone ring. She strained her ears to listen as the speaker started to leave a message.

"Hi Ella. It's Uncle Lionel. I was wondering if you could do me a favor and take a drive over to the cottage and open it up for me. I've got it rented out for the summer, and your Aunt Joan and I haven't had a chance to get up there yet. Call me back if there's a problem okay, hon? Thanks."

She suddenly felt dismal. If her aunt and uncle had rented out their cottage then they weren't going to spend the summer here themselves. Usually she could count on having her family show up as soon as the weather turned warm and the mosquito population thinned out. But it now appeared she would be on her own this year.

"Mommy, can we eat?" yelled Calvin from his bedroom.

Ella shook off her desolate thoughts and headed to the kitchen. "Just give me a few minutes to whip something up, okay, sweetie?" she called to Calvin. She could hear him while she opened the cupboards and tried to figure out what to make for dinner.

"Hurry, Mommy. I hungry."

She took her mind off things after they ate by tidying up the house and throwing in a load of laundry. She folded what was in the dryer, then washed up a sink full of dishes by hand because her dishwasher had quit on her soon after Joe had died. Before she knew it, it was time to give Calvin a bath. Afterward she read him two stories and tucked him into bed before collapsing in front of the television to catch some of the news.

She went to bed around ten-thirty and lay awake, pondering her dire straits. She hadn't called her uncle back because she'd not wanted to hear him tell her that no one would be up to visit the cottage this summer. Her fear was that if she heard the actual words she might just break down and cry. After her meeting at the bank, she had felt rejected enough for the day. She finally drifted off, falling into a blissful sleep, dreaming of winning a fortune in the lottery.

~*~

"Mommy, wake up. Time to get out of bed."

Ella groaned as her bed began to shake, Calvin bouncing excitedly upon it. She reached out and pulled him down into her arms for a hug. "Morning, sweetie pie."

He giggled at the silly name she called him as he cuddled up beside her. "I'm not a pie, Mommy. I'm a boy."

"Yes, you are. You're a big boy, aren't you?"

11

"Yes, me am big."

"*I* am big," Ella corrected.

"Me too," Calvin laughed, then struggled out of her embrace. He reached out to pull her hand from the side of the bed where he now stood. "Come on, Mommy. Time to get up."

Ella groaned. It couldn't possibly be seven o'clock already. She turned her head to peer at the alarm clock and groaned again. It was seven. She felt as though she'd just fallen asleep. Dragging herself out of bed, she dressed and went into the kitchen, where Calvin had already seated himself at the table.

"I hungry, Mommy."

"What would you like to eat this morning, my sweet?"

"Yes. Sweets."

"No. How about some cereal?" she asked, reaching into the cupboard.

"Don't want cereal. Want French toast."

Ella sighed. "Sorry babe. We don't have any eggs left."

"French toast," Calvin insisted, glaring at the bowl she placed in front of him.

"Come on, now. If you eat up your cereal like a big boy, I'll buy you some cookies at the grocery store, okay?"

"Okay," he yelled, excited about the treat.

Calvin ate his cereal while Ella sipped coffee and forced down a piece of toast. Her stomach felt clenched in fright this morning, and she knew she was worried about not getting the loan.

She made a mental note to head over to her uncle's cottage after she'd finished with groceries. She put her forlorn thoughts aside about not seeing her family. Instead, she decided, she would call her aunt and ask if perhaps her cousins could come and stay at her house for a visit.

Ella lifted Calvin down from his car seat after finding a parking spot at the grocery store. She hated shopping, especially when she knew how things would go once they got inside the store. Calvin would ask for something and she would have to deny him, and the tantrums would begin. It was the reason she shopped as early as possible. Foregoing the extra hour of sleep she could get on a Saturday morning, as few people as possible would have to witness her son's hysterics. She wished she could buy him the things he asked for, because they weren't extravagant demands. Something as simple as a box of cereal with a toy in it was his customary request. Unfortunately, it was usually too expensive, unless by some miracle it was on sale.

Sure enough, it was as she feared. Creeping slowly down the cereal aisle with Calvin walking beside her, there wasn't a sale in sight. They made a once over sweep of the aisle, her scanning all of the prices, Calvin checking out all of the prizes. As she swung the cart back around to take another look, Calvin saw something he liked.

"I want this one," he exclaimed, grabbing onto the box and holding it tight against his chest.

Ella checked the price and noted with dismay that he'd grabbed the most expensive box of cereal on the shelf. She looked at her son's face, taking in the tight grim line of his mouth as he prepared to do battle. Thankfully, no one else was yet in the aisle to witness her embarrassment as she leaned down and spoke softly to him. "Sweetheart, remember the talk we had about cereal last week?"

"I don't care if it's too 'spensive, Mommy. I *have* to have this one. Look, it has a watch inside, and I'm a big boy so I need one. You said I was big, 'member?"

"Yes, you are big. Big enough to not cry and yell in the store, right?"

"But you said I could have a treat if I ate my cereal this morning."

"I said that I would get you some cookies."

"Don't want cookies. Want cereal with a watch in it!"

Calvin had yelled the last few words, and Ella knew that look on his face all too well. He was about to lose control. Thank God she had chosen this aisle second to last—she was almost finished with her shopping. She tried to gently pry the box from his hands, but he refused to relinquish his hold. To her embarrassment, they wound up in a tug-a-war. She bent down in a crouch as she tugged.

Calvin's expression changed suddenly. He no longer looked at her—his sights were now focused on something behind her. He abruptly let go of the box and Ella, who had still been pulling, fell over backward onto the floor. She had spun around as she fell and now, to her supreme embarrassment, realized they were no longer alone in the aisle. Before her eyes were a large pair of men's shoes, and she feared in that instant the manager of the store had come to throw them out.

She lay sprawled there, frozen with shame over the way she must look to this man. She wondered if he had seen her engaged in a tug-a-war with her child, and she could just imagine what he must be thinking. His hand came into view, reaching down to aid her in rising. She tentatively placed her hand in his and allowed him to raise her to her feet. Once she stood before him she slowly lifted her gaze to his face. Instead of the censure she expected, she saw a slight smile and a gleam in his eye. It wasn't the store manager, but a stranger she had never seen before in this small town.

"Are you all right?" he asked.

Ella was mesmerized by the kind look on his handsome face. "Ah, yes. Thank you."

"Good," he replied, his mouth breaking into a large grin. "I see you won."

"I won?" she asked, confused. Then she followed his gaze to the floor and noted the box of cereal at her feet. She immediately turned a bright shade of red.

Calvin came up beside her at that moment. He reached down and picked up the cereal to put it back on the shelf. "Sorry, Mommy," he said. He looked up at the man, who loomed like a giant before him. "Why are you so big?" he asked.

"Calvin," she scolded. "It's impolite to ask questions like that."

"Well, he is big."

And indeed he was, Ella noted. Big and broad. He was built like a football player or a fireman. Though he was dressed neatly in black jeans and a short-sleeved blue shirt, she couldn't help but notice the way his muscles bulged through his clothes. He must be well over six feet tall, she surmised, considering he towered over her own five-and-a-half-foot frame. In contrast with his overbearing size, his face was gentle, and so was his hand when he had helped her to her feet. His hair was a lighter brown than her own, and she guessed if he untied it from the ponytail he sported, it might be as long as hers, which just brushed against her shoulders. His eyes were the deepest blue she had ever seen, making her brown ones seem plain. When she realized she was staring, she quickly turned her face downward to look at Calvin. The man remained before her, and she suddenly felt slightly uncomfortable.

"I'll let you get back to your shopping," he said, breaking the silence.

He stepped away from her and made his way around Calvin and their shopping cart. Ella watched him walk down the length of the aisle, wanting to say something to him but not knowing what. Soon he disappeared, and she distractedly grabbed a box of puffed wheat from the shelf and tossed it into the cart. Calvin didn't utter a word of protest.

She let him pick out a small box of inexpensive cookies, then they checked out and she guided the cart towards her car. After buckling Calvin into his car seat, she opened the trunk and began to load the groceries inside. It must have been fate, for the next thing she knew, the stranger from the grocery store walked up to the car beside hers. He gave her a slight nod as he unlocked the trunk of his black sports car and went to put his own bags of groceries within. She couldn't help but peer over at him. He didn't say anything to her, nor did he look her way again—that was, until one of her bags broke and a bunch of tin cans fell to the ground and began to roll in every direction.

"Oh no," she exclaimed, making a scramble to grab them. She knelt on the ground and reached far underneath her car for a still rolling can of tuna. As she climbed to her feet she noticed the man had captured some of the wayward cans. He stood before her, wearing that large grin on his face again. When he passed them over to her she mumbled an awkward "Thanks" as she took them from his hands.

It figured, she thought with dismay, if she was going to make a complete fool out of herself, it had to be in front of one of the cutest guys she'd ever seen.

"I'll take that back for you," he offered, gesturing toward the cart.

"Thank you, that'd be great," Ella replied. She watched him walk away with her cart as she slammed down the trunk and climbed inside the car. She drove past him as she went to pull out of the lot and gave him a brief wave. He smiled and waved in return.

At home, she carried in the groceries and put them on the kitchen floor. Calvin reached inside the bags and began pulling out the items and stacking them on the counter. Ella went outside to retrieve the loose cans, and as she came back inside she heard Calvin squeal in delight.

"Thank you, Mommy! Thank you!" he yelled, as he barreled toward her and grabbed her around the legs in a bear hug.

"What's that for?" she asked, smiling down at him, trying to keep the cans from slipping from her grasp. Calvin finally let go and ran back into the kitchen. Ella entered just in time to see him rip open the top of the box of cereal they had argued over. She was shocked and searched her memory for how it could have gotten into one of her bags. And then she remembered. The man at the store. He had seen them tugging it back and forth, and he must have bought it for Calvin. When she had leaned down for the can under her car, he must have slipped it into one of the bags in her trunk. But why would he do it? she wondered as she watched Calvin pull out the watch and shake it triumphantly in the air.

Ella didn't let on to Calvin that it had been the man at the store who had bought him the cereal. She let him believe it was her. She assured herself it was the right thing to do, because time and again she had told him not to accept anything from a stranger. Never mind that she was breaking her own rule. It was also too embarrassing to admit, even to her son, that the man had probably felt sorry for them. No doubt the reason he had done what he did.

She quickly put away the groceries and then buckled Calvin into the car to make the drive out to the cottage. Every few minutes he would relay to Ella what the numbers on his watch read. She could hear the pride in his voice, as he believed he was actually telling the time, his excitement evident in his newly discovered talent.

Uncle Lionel had not said in his message what day the renters would be arriving to take possession of the cottage. He'd only said that it was rented for the summer. Perhaps they would be here on Monday, she thought. It wouldn't give her much time to tidy up. She might have to spend the rest of her weekend doing a spring cleaning.

"Almost there, Mommy," Calvin declared, peering intently at his watch.

They had turned off the roadway out of town and onto a dirt road that would lead to the lake. About two dozen cottages were nestled around the water's edge. The lake was named Loon, which suited it perfectly seeing as how several pairs of loons had taken up residence there.

A few minutes later, after following the many twists and turns in the road, they pulled up in front of her uncle's cottage.

"We're here, Mommy. Just in time," Calvin stated, tapping a finger to his watch.

Ella lifted him out of the car seat and wondered how long his preoccupation with that watch of his would last. She watched him rush around to the front of the cottage, which faced the lake, as soon as his feet hit the ground. He loved to climb up the stairs of the big deck and look out toward the water.

Ella went into the cottage through the back door and then walked across the living room to open the other door for Calvin. Then she went into the bedroom that had the electrical panel in it and pushed up the power bar, bringing electricity into the cottage. She surveyed the living room after pulling open the curtains that covered the windows, and then made her way around through the kitchen and each of the four bedrooms to open those curtains as well. The cottage was dusty but otherwise quite tidy. It just needed a bit of airing out, she decided, as she went about sliding open a few windows.

After completing the tedious task of climbing underneath the cottage and priming the pump, she went inside to turn off all of the faucets, which were now gushing water. She leaned under the kitchen sink and grabbed a cloth for dusting and began walking around wiping surfaces. Calvin had come inside and dragged a child-sized lawn chair from one of the bedrooms out onto the deck. Ella wished she could join him outside instead of being stuck dusting on such a beautiful day. She worked quickly though, and soon was outside on the deck shaking away the inevitable mouse droppings from the blankets in the linen closet.

She gazed toward the lake and could see the sparkle of the sun as it reflected off the water's surface. The ever-present loons were splashing about and calling out to one another. It was too bad, she reflected, that the place was rented out. She wouldn't have minded spending a couple of days here with Calvin. Her own house was peaceful like this, but the view wasn't the same. The lake seemed to lend an air of tranquility.

Ella didn't see why they couldn't spend a little time relaxing on the deck, however, or perhaps they could go out in the paddleboat for a while. Calvin was always enthusiastic about peddling the boat with his little feet. The canoe her uncle owned was also fun to use, but it proved to be much more work for her considering that Calvin was still trying to get used to using a paddle. She remembered how she and Joe used to take Calvin out for hours in the boats. They had explored the other side of the lake, hiking far into the woods with a picnic lunch. Ella felt a sudden wave of nostalgia wash over her. Maybe it wasn't such a good idea after all, she sighed.

Chapter Two

"Mommy, what-cha thinkin'?" Calvin asked.

Ella shook from her reverie and pasted a large, if somewhat phony, smile on her face. "I'm thinking it would be nice if we went out for a ride in the paddle boat."

Her suggestion brought an immediate whoop of joy from Calvin. He jumped to his feet and rushed past her to throw open the screen door.

"I'll get the life jackets!" he hollered as he ran inside.

She leaned on the railing of the deck while she waited for Calvin to return. Leaving the cottage windows open for a while would give it time to air out, and it was a beautiful day for a boat ride, she assured herself, putting her doubts aside.

"Can't find the jackets, Mommy," Calvin yelled through the open window.

"I'll help you."

Once inside, she headed down the hallway to the last bedroom and searched through the closet where the jackets

21

were usually stored. Calvin sat at the end of the bed and informed her he had already looked in there. Reaching up to move aside an air mattress, she suddenly froze as she heard the back door of the cottage open. She'd closed it after she entered, and knew it was that door because it gave a loud squeak when opened.

She turned to Calvin and put her finger against her lips in a gesture to keep him silent. The room they were in had a single bed in it and also a bunk bed. She lifted Calvin from the single bed, and with some effort heaved him up over her head onto the top of the bunk-bed.

"Lie down against the wall and don't move," she whispered sternly, letting him know she would take no nonsense from him. Calvin must have sensed the seriousness of the situation and did as she asked.

Seeing that her son was hidden from sight, Ella walked toward the door of the bedroom and stepped into the hallway, silently pulling the door shut behind her. It was probably just one of the neighbors from the lake, she told herself as she began creeping toward the other end of the cottage, but she would take no chances when it came to her son's safety.

Approaching the end of the hall, Ella stopped and pressed herself against the wall. She took a deep breath before chancing a peek around the corner toward the kitchen and the back door. To her dismay, there stood a large hulking form of a man. He had his back to her as he placed something in his hands onto the kitchen table. After releasing his burden, he turned and walked to the door and then, to her relief, stepped outside.

As soon as he left, she ran back down the hallway and

threw open the bedroom door. She lifted her hands up to Calvin, and when he dove into her arms she wasted no time rushing toward the front door. Holding tightly to her son, she hoped she could make it out in time, thinking if she hurried she could escape before the man came back inside and discovered them. She still didn't know if he posed a threat to them or not, but it was better, she knew, to be safe than sorry.

Unfortunately, as she grappled with the door handle with one hand, still holding tight to Calvin with the other, she heard the screen of the back door squeak open. Instead of giving in, Ella doubled her efforts and finally flung the door wide. As she made ready to flee, a deep voice came from behind her.

"Hey! Stop!"

Ella didn't stop. She barreled outside onto the deck, and was just nearing the stairs when she felt a strong hand grasp her by the arm. Though firm, the grip was not cruel, as the man turned her, shaking and frightened, toward him.

"Don't hurt my son!" she cried, trying desperately to shield Calvin with her body.

The man let go of her immediately and stepped back. She increased the distance between them before she finally lifted her gaze to look at him. His face, though shocked, she noted, perhaps from her words, was familiar to her. In fact, as she peered more closely at him, recognition finally set in. It was the man from the grocery store. She became more afraid with this realization, for what would he be doing here if not following her and Calvin?

"What do you want?" Ella demanded, trying to make her voice fierce and strong though she shivered like a wet kitten.

The man must have noticed by the way she clung

23

protectively to her child that she feared him. He splayed his hands out before her in a gesture of innocence. "I'm not going to hurt you," he said gently.

"Why are you following us?" Anger was slowly beginning to replace her panic as she felt Calvin's little body shaking with fright.

"I'm not following you," he said.

"Then it's a mighty big coincidence that you're here!"

"I'm renting this cottage. That's why I'm here."

"You're renting my uncle's cottage?" she asked with disbelief.

"Your uncle's cottage?" Confusion, then a look of understanding passed over his face. "So that's what you're doing here. For a moment, I thought you were following *me*."

"That's absurd," Ella insisted, stunned by his words.

"It wouldn't be the first time," he stated.

She stared at him as though he were crazy. "And how long have you deluded yourself with the fact that you're so incredibly irresistible?"

He appeared shocked over that statement. "But people do follow me."

"Why would they do that?" Ella scoffed.

"You mean you really don't know who I am?" His voice held a touch of arrogance and disbelief.

"Should I?"

"I'm Gabriel Stolks."

Even if Ella hadn't worked in a library and known of several famous authors, she probably still would have recognized the name. Gabriel Stolks was one of the best-known mystery writers in the country. Even in a small town

SEND ME AN ANGEL

like Caverly, his name would be hard pressed not to be well known. The thing about authors, though, was that no matter how famous they were, they could still get around without a lot of fanfare because many of their faces weren't familiar. Even if they were as famous as Gabriel Stolks.

"How do I know you're really him?" Ella asked.

Calvin had started to struggle, so she placed him on his feet but gently pushed him behind her.

He soon became curious and peeked around her legs at the man before them, who was becoming irritated.

"Well, how do I know this is really your uncle's cottage?" he challenged her.

"Hey Mommy, it's the man from the cereal aisle," Calvin exclaimed, recalling the man they'd seen this morning.

Ella inwardly cringed, suddenly remembering that this man had concealed a box of expensive cereal in her trunk. What was worse was that her son was wearing the evidence of his charitable gesture.

"I can prove who I am," she told him. "Just look inside— there's a picture of my son and me on the end table in the living room."

She was slightly surprised when he did just that. He went inside, and before she regained her senses and realized she could now flee, he came back out. In his hands he held a book. Not just any book though—it was one written by Gabriel Stolks. He handed it over to her with the back flap lying open. Her hands began to tremble as she looked at the picture of the man who now stood before her.

"It is you."

"To be fair, I saw your picture inside."

Ella laughed. She was embarrassed and relieved at the same time. She didn't know if she should try to make a graceful exit or ask him for his autograph.

"I'm, ah...sorry about this...Mr. Stolks," she stammered.

He smiled at her kindly. "It's all right. I'm the one who should apologize for frightening you."

"My uncle asked me to come here and get the place ready for a renter, but I never could have imagined...." She trailed off, shocked that such a famous writer was standing before her.

"I take it you weren't expecting me to arrive today?"

"I really wasn't sure when you were coming. Or who, for that matter, was coming. I just assumed it would be on Monday."

"I would have been here an hour ago, but unfortunately, I got lost on the road from town. Oh!" he exclaimed suddenly. "I forgot I bought milk at the store. If I don't get it into a refrigerator soon I'll have to go back for more. Excuse me a moment," he said, rushing inside.

With the mention of the grocery store, Ella began to feel uncomfortable again. Her anxiety increased when Calvin said, "Mommy, it's time for our boat ride."

She looked down at her son, and to her dismay he was tapping on that watch of his again.

"Calvin, sweetheart, I'm sorry, but I don't think we'll be able to take a boat ride after all."

"But I want to take a boat ride, Mommy. You said we could," Calvin whined loudly.

She felt torn. She didn't want to disappoint Calvin, but she also didn't want to intrude on Mr. Stolks's time any longer.

She knelt down before her son, hoping to get him to cooperate with her instead of putting up a fight. But before she could say anything, she heard Mr. Stolks come back outside and walk up to stand behind her.

"What's this about a boat ride, young man?" he asked Calvin seriously, having overheard the boy's words. "Are you offering your services as my guide around the lake this morning?"

"Oh, no. He couldn't possibly—," Ella began, only to be cut off by Calvin's enthusiastic response.

"Yes. I can be your guide, mister. I know my way around this lake better 'n anybody."

Gabriel darted a quick look toward Ella while hearing Calvin's boast. "Well, it's all settled then—that is, if it's all right with your mom?" He directed his question to Calvin, but his eyes were still on Ella.

Ella quickly rose to her feet. "Really, Mr. Stolks—," she began.

"Gabriel, please," he insisted. "I didn't catch your name, by the way."

"Oh," she exclaimed, remembering her manners. "I'm sorry. I'm Ella Tolomy, and this little fellow is Calvin."

"It's a pleasure to make your acquaintance," he announced formally, then broke into a broad grin. "Now, what do you say? Could you spare some time for the new guy in town and give him a little tour?"

He asked so nicely, and Calvin seemed so excited over the prospect of being a guide, Ella felt she was out-numbered.

"Oh, why not? But just for a little while, all right?"

"Okay!" Calvin exclaimed, then he said, "Mommy, we

couldn't find the life jackets,

'member?"

Ah, she thought, *I might just get out of this yet.* It wasn't that she was anxious to get away from Gabriel; it was only that she needed time to gather her wits. She felt as though she'd been through the spin cycle of her washer.

"I noticed there was a little shed by the water when I drove up. Maybe the jackets are in there," Gabriel suggested.

"Let's go look," Calvin yelled, and dashed toward the end of the deck to hurry down the steps.

"Slow down, Calvin. Let me come with you," Ella insisted, quickly heading after him.

"I'll grab us a little something to eat for lunch," Gabriel offered.

Before she could tell him that she didn't intend for them to be gone long enough to need supplies, he had turned and walked inside. She couldn't go after him; Calvin was already nearing the shed, and she couldn't leave him alone so close to the water. She hesitated for only a moment before running after her son, wondering along the way what she'd gotten herself into.

They found the jackets in the shed, but Calvin refused to enter to grab them. It seemed some spiders had been busy and their sticky webs dangled before the doorway. Ella eyed the offending strands and searched around for a stick to move them aside. She cleared most of them away before Calvin bravely declared that he could make it in now, acting as if it were some daring escapade he was attempting. Hurrying into the shed, he snatched up two adult jackets and a smaller one for himself. He barreled out of there quickly and tossed the jackets to the ground just as Gabriel walked over from the cottage to join them.

He carried a wicker picnic basket and had a folded blanket swung over his arm. When he saw the jackets on the ground he put down the basket and lay the blanket on top of it. Shaking off the little jacket, he handed it to Calvin and asked him if he'd like to demonstrate how to put it on. Feeling important, Calvin was quick to take the jacket from Gabriel's hands and went about explaining how one should wear it. "Slip your arms into these holes, see?" he said, putting on the jacket. "Then after you zip it up, you use this buckle here to snap the sides together. Like this."

Gabriel had picked up the larger jacket and followed along with Calvin's instructions, appearing to pay strict attention. Ella had to turn her head away so Calvin wouldn't see how amusing she found his little show. She donned her own jacket, then searched about in the shed for some paddles for the canoe. They wouldn't be able to take the paddleboat, as it only seated two people. She didn't think Calvin would be disappointed though, considering how much he was enjoying displaying his considerable skills.

Ella had Gabriel help her remove the tarp from the canoe and flip it over before they carried it to the water. Calvin stood back and fired instructions at them while they did the job. Minutes later, Ella was climbing aboard the boat and then helping Calvin onto the middle seat. Gabriel handed down the picnic basket and blanket to her before he pushed them away from the shore and claimed his own seat.

Ella sighed as they sailed smoothly out into the bay. The water was calm and quiet. No motorboats were allowed on

Loon Lake, so they were spared the unsettling waves and noise of bigger boats rushing by. The surface of the small lake was flat, only breaking when a fish jumped to grab an insect floating by. Of course, there were the ever-present loons, enjoying a late morning frolic by the water's edge. Calvin and his observations soon broke the peacefulness however.

"That only took us seven minutes, Mommy," he yelled, his loud voice echoing around the lake.

Ella's shoulders slumped. It was a good thing, she thought, that her back was to Gabriel and he couldn't see how red her face had become. Why hadn't she tried harder to get out of this boat ride, she mentally berated herself. Now she had to endure at least the next hour with Calvin announcing the time every five minutes, and she would have to keep reliving the humiliation of this morning's fiasco.

"What kind of fish can you find in this lake, Calvin?" Gabriel asked.

Ella sighed, filled with gratitude for the distraction his question brought about.

Calvin was thoughtful for a moment before he responded. "There's bass, and sunfish. If you're lucky, you may catch a pike or even a catfish — they're cool 'cause they have whiskers. And, there's also tons and tons of rock bass."

"What kind of bait would you recommend?"

"Well, Uncle Lionel likes to use minnows or worms, but Mommy only uses lures 'cause she says worms make her hands smelly."

"Hmm, I'll keep that in mind," Gabriel said.

Calvin then pointed out the best places to catch bass and the elusive pike while Gabriel paid strict attention.

Ella told him where the sand bar was, and pointed out some large and somewhat dangerous rocks to avoid that hid just beneath the surface. She also informed him where to find the trail to see a beautiful waterfall, and another which led to a different lake. Before they knew it, it was time to eat. At least, according to Calvin's watch it was.

Calvin's fingers dangled in the water as Gabriel maneuvered the canoe over to a rock face, which the sun beat upon, protruding out into the lake. Calvin had chosen this spot and insisted they have their picnic there.

As Ella stepped ashore and tied off the boat, she looked about fondly. Her memories of this place were bittersweet. She and Joe had often sat upon this very rock and shared special talks together. After Calvin was born they had brought him here and enjoyed family picnics and hikes on the trail beyond the rock.

"Where would you like to lay the blanket, Ella?" Gabriel asked, interrupting her thoughts.

"Oh," she said. "How about right over there?"

Gabriel smiled and gave her a nod before walking over to the spot she had indicated. He lay the blanket across the smooth rock, then placed the basket on it. He opened it and began handing items to Calvin, who had come over to help him. Ella joined the pair and sat down alongside her son. She looked at the food that Gabriel had quickly packed up for them and was impressed.

He'd brought lunchmeat and cheese, and a long stick of fresh French bread that he must have bought this morning in town. When she thought the basket was empty he reached in again and brought out grapes, three golden apples, and pound

31

cake for dessert. To drink he'd packed a bottle of pear cider. Calvin seemed to feel very grown up when Gabriel poured it into three small plastic wineglasses that he unpacked and passed one to him.

"It's not real wine," Gabriel whispered to Ella, when she raised an eyebrow at him.

"I know, it's just that you shouldn't have gone to so much trouble," she insisted, as Gabriel reached into the basket for a knife. Ella took it from his hand and began cutting up the bread.

She gave a piece to Calvin and he started piling on meat and cheese.

"It's the least I can do, considering how you've taken the time to show me around. It's very kind of you."

Calvin ignored their polite conversation as he devoured his sandwich and then started stuffing grapes into his mouth.

"These are good, Mommy. Why don't you ever buy grapes?" he asked between mouthfuls, to Ella's embarrassment.

She didn't want to tell Calvin in front of Gabriel that it was because she couldn't afford to buy special fruit. She always bought apples — red ones though, not the expensive golden ones that Gabriel had brought. Oranges and bananas were usually reasonable, so she bought those every week as well. She couldn't remember the last time they'd had cantaloupe or kiwi or even watermelon, never mind grapes.

Gabriel was watching Calvin stuff himself, making it appear as though he hadn't had a decent meal in ages. Ella feared that was exactly what the man was thinking. It had probably been the reason he had suggested this little sojourn, she surmised, recalling how quickly he had dashed off to pack up lunch. Just as he had bought the cereal for Calvin, now he was plying him with fancy fruit because he knew she couldn't. Did he think she would feel grateful to him? That she should thank him for his generosity toward her and her son? Was this his good deed for the day?

The bite of French bread in her mouth suddenly tasted like cardboard, and she had to drink some of the pear cider just to force it down. Ella felt a wave of bitterness wash over her. This felt like a betrayal somehow, to her husband's memory. It should be Joe sitting here with her and Calvin, not some stranger who felt sorry for them. This was her family's special spot, and here they were sharing it with a man they'd just met this morning.

Gabriel must have noticed the shadow that crossed her face, as he tried to lighten the mood by speaking with Calvin. "I saw signs in town about an annual jamboree in a couple of weeks — it looks like fun. Are you going to go?"

Calvin seemed to consider his answer for a moment, which gave him a chance to eat another grape. "I know we used to go, but we haven't been since my daddy went to Heaven."

Gabriel appeared momentarily startled by this bit of information, but quickly masked his surprise. Ella had just assumed he knew she was a widow, but how could he as she'd never offered him that bit of information?

"My husband was killed in an accident over two years ago," she explained.

"I'm sorry," he replied, seeming to not know what else to say.

He gazed at her strangely, but it wasn't with the pity she'd expected. For a moment, Ella thought she detected a glimmer of something else. He looked at her the way a man looks at a woman. She held his gaze and then quickly looked away. It had been a long time since she had gained the attention of a man. She was a mother, but she was also a woman. A woman who had been alone for a long time and sometimes ached with longing to feel strong arms around her, protecting and cherishing her. But she had no right to feel this way, she reminded herself, not here in this place or with this man. This place belonged to her and Joe, and their child. The only problem was Joe was gone, and she had to go on without him.

"Mommy, I drank too much juice." Calvin was suddenly up and doing a little dance.

Ella sprang to her feet, and she could hear Gabriel chuckle as she hurried Calvin off into the bushes. When they returned she helped him pack up what remained of their lunch and fold the blanket. As she set the basket into the canoe Gabriel spotted the trail and wandered over to stand before it.

"Is this the trail you said leads to the other lake?" he asked her.

"Yes."

"How far away is it? I'd like to go. Not today, but perhaps next week."

"You can't go there alone, you'd get lost," Calvin informed him.

"The walk is over an hour, and unfortunately, Calvin is correct. You really shouldn't risk heading out alone because the trail is very tricky to follow."

"Sounds like another job for my guide, then," Gabriel said to Calvin.

Before Calvin could jump all over with excitement, Ella had to reluctantly burst his bubble.

"I'm sorry, Gabriel, but Calvin will be at his sitter's house through the week because I have to go to work."

"I see," he said. "Then how about next Saturday?"

"Okay!" yelled Calvin.

"I don't know," Ella said, searching her mind to come up with an excuse even though she knew she didn't have any plans. She didn't want to spend any more time with Gabriel. Being with him reminded her of how much it hurt to be alone. Yes, he was going to be around all summer, and maybe they could spend time together. But then he would leave, and Ella didn't think she had it in her to go through another loss. It was better to not get close to him at all, she told herself.

He was staring at her intently, and so was Calvin, waiting for her answer. Her son was so hopeful as he regarded her. She couldn't allow it, she determined, not only for her sake but for Calvin's as well. She saw the way he was beginning to admire Gabriel. If she ended it now, it would be better for him.

But she couldn't say the words.

It was as though time had stopped and would not resume until she did. Just one word, a word to spare her son and herself from any future heartbreak. One word to dash Calvin's hopes to the earth. She couldn't do it. Looking at her son's face, she could not say no.

"How about ten o'clock?" she finally said.

"Ten would be great!" Calvin yelled, tapping his watch.

Chapter Three

During the drive home Ella was barely aware of what Calvin chattered about. She had mixed feelings over what had happened today, and she needed time alone to process the events.

If ever in her life she had felt confused and uncertain of what to do, now was the time. She had liked being with Gabriel, and she knew that Calvin had enjoyed himself. It had been so long since they had spent time with a man other than her Uncle Lionel.

Oh, yes—Uncle Lionel. The devil! She was willing to bet that he was certain she would run into Gabriel when he sent her to the cottage. She had noticed Gabriel didn't wear a wedding ring, and she'd given him ample time to admit that he had a significant other. No, she surmised, Gabriel must not be married or involved with anyone. Uncle Lionel had done his homework.

One year after Joe's death he had started in on her about

finding someone else. "You're too young to sit on the shelf," he'd told her. She hadn't confessed to him how afraid she was to date, only telling him she wasn't quite ready yet.

She pulled into her driveway not much later, and was surprised to see that Calvin had fallen asleep. She unfastened him from his car seat and carried him inside. Putting him down in his bed, she figured he was worn out by this morning's adventures.

With Calvin asleep, Ella was suddenly unsure of what to do with her time. She ventured into the yard, leaving the back door open so if Calvin awoke he would know where she was. She pulled weeds from the vegetable garden, then grabbed a bowl from inside to pick some of the green beans that had begun to sprout. Her garden supplied them with a bounty of fresh vegetables throughout the season, and the flower garden filled their home with sweet smells of spring and summer. This was what she would miss the most, Ella decided with a heavy heart, if she was forced to sell her home. Calvin also loved their yard, which gave him lots of room to run and play as little boys should. She couldn't imagine how he would adapt to the confines of an apartment with his endless supply of energy.

At dinner that night, she served up chicken and potatoes with green beans on the side. Calvin made a face as she piled them onto his plate, taking for granted the harvested rewards of her labor.

"Hate beans. Want more grapes," he told her.

"These are special beans from Mommy's own garden," Ella informed him, ignoring how he pushed them off to the far side of his plate with a fork.

"Don't like chicken either."

"I was hoping you'd be more agreeable after your nap."

Calvin scowled at her remark, reminding him of his humiliation of drifting off to sleep in the car. "Only babies take naps."

"You had a hard day at work today—you needed to take a nap."

"Work?" he asked, automatically sitting up straighter and paying attention.

"Yes, as a guide," Ella reminded him.

His face took on a look of glee as he no doubt recalled how he'd been the one to boss around the grown-ups this morning. "Gab-real was sure happy for my help, Mommy."

Ella's impressed expression was tightly controlled; she dare not betray the slightest hint of a smile. "He certainly was."

Calvin's chest puffed out and he stabbed his fork into one of the green beans. "Guess I need my strength, if I gotta show him 'round next week too," he sighed dramatically.

Ella sat down to eat her own dinner and watched as Calvin cleaned his entire plate. When he was finished, he drank down his milk. Then he showed her his muscles and said he was off to draw a map for next week's hike.

She called Uncle Lionel after Calvin went to bed.

"How did everything go at the cottage?" he asked her, trying to keep his voice casual.

"Don't you mean, how did I get along with Gabriel Stolks?"

"Oh, good. So you did meet after all?"

"Wasn't that what you'd planned all along?" She could

hear her uncle's light chuckle, and she couldn't help but feel annoyed. "You should have prepared me. You caused us both a lot of embarrassment, not to mention shock. I was terrified when he walked in, and so was Calvin."

"Oh, dear. I'm sorry. I didn't mean for it to happen that way," he said, truly contrite.

"Please, Uncle Lionel, no more matchmaking, all right? Besides, Gabriel's way out of my league. He's a famous author, and I'm a nobody."

"Nonsense. You're an intelligent, beautiful young lady," he insisted.

"I'm a widow with a young son who lives in the boonies." The line was silent for a moment, and she knew he was taking a deep breath so he wouldn't continue to argue with her. They'd had this conversation a hundred times, and it always ended with Ella having the last word.

He changed the topic instead. "I left Mr. Stolks your home phone number on a note of instructions at the cottage. If he needs help with anything, I indicated that he call you because you're nearby. Okay?"

"I'm sure he'll be fine," she told him, not wanting to mention that she and Calvin were planning on taking Gabriel up to Bethower Lake next Saturday. He would just read more into it than being a simple hike, and she didn't want to get his hopes up.

"Is everything okay, honey?" he asked her. "You sound a little sad tonight."

Actually, she was still feeling down about not getting the money from the bank, and she guessed he could detect that in her voice. She tried to sound more upbeat. "Everything's fine.

It's late, and you know what Calvin's like. He's just tired me out." Then she remembered how she'd wanted to ask if her cousins would like to come for a visit this summer. "I guess I'm also disappointed that you and Aunt Joan aren't coming up. Do you think it would be all right if Jen and Katherine spent some time at my house? I know Calvin would love it."

"I think they'd jump at the chance to get out of the city for a while. I'll talk it over with them and let you know, okay?"

After bidding her uncle a good night, Ella felt slightly better. At least she may soon have her cousins around to distract her from her troubles.

Sunday morning was spent at church. A beautiful white chapel sat atop a hill in Caverly's town, with steps winding up to it from the sidewalk. Ella had been enchanted since she'd first laid eyes upon it.

It was a comfort to her to be surrounded by the people of Caverly while she and Calvin attended church as they had when Joe was alive. In some way, it made her feel closer to Joe, who most of them had known since his early childhood. He had grown up in this small friendly town, and taken over his father's business after the death of his parents. She had spent many summers in Caverly at her uncle's cottage, but did not meet Joe until she'd come up to spend some time alone here at the age of eighteen. She'd been in the town's only pub one evening and Joe had come in after work. Once they'd laid eyes on each other it had been love at first sight. Joe had been her summer love for the next two years, but come the fall she had always returned to the city and her parents' home.

And then tragedy struck. At the age of twenty, Ella's parents were both killed in a plane crash. She had gone up north to recover from the loss and had found comfort in Joe's embrace.

Joe had been her anchor, for having lost his own parents he could well understand her grief. And in the midst of all of her sadness there had been a light, for Joe proposed to her that summer and asked her to come and live with him. He had even offered her a job as his secretary in his small business. She had quickly agreed, for there was no longer anything keeping her in the city. Their wedding in the small white chapel had been a quiet affair. Joe had no family but his many friends had attended, and Ella's Aunt Joan and Uncle Lionel, along with her two younger cousins, Jenny and Katherine, had made the trip in for the service.

Ella dropped Calvin off at Sunday school in the basement with the other young children before entering the service room in the church. The only seats available were at the back with Mrs. Hanks and Mrs. Tine. It was her own fault for coming in late; she would have to sit with the two gossiping widows.

"Ella! It's been ages since we talked," Mrs. Tine said, patting the seat beside her.

Ella sighed and sat down.

"Have you heard that Darren has been up to his old tricks again?" Mrs. Hanks said, leaning over her friend to talk to Ella. Darren Aveley ran a sporting goods store in town, which was closed more often than open due to his drinking habit. Ella didn't know how he managed to stay in business.

"No, I haven't heard anything," Ella said, knowing whether she had heard the story or not, she was going to hear it again anyway.

Through most of the service the two older ladies filled

41

Ella in on all the goings-on with everyone in town. Their tones were hushed, but no less delighted in what they deemed their obligation to keep Ella informed. Ella nodded politely during the prattle, but was careful to not add to the gossip or to reveal any details of her own life lest it become public knowledge.

At the end of the service, Ella waited for Calvin to rejoin her before they made their way out past the minister, who shook hands and offered warm smiles to everyone. Bypassing the crowd that gathered beneath the cloudless sky to socialize, Ella hurried down the steps to her car. She held tight to Calvin's hand while successfully declining offers of lunch at a restaurant in town made by some of Joe's old friends.

"Why don't we eat in town anymore, Mommy?" Calvin asked as she lifted him into his car seat.

"I'd rather eat at home," she told him.

Calvin sat at the picnic table outside for most of the afternoon, working on his map while Ella puttered around in her garden. She took advantage of the beautiful warm day to enjoy the out-of-doors, knowing she would soon be stuck inside at work. At least Calvin could spend his time playing outside with Mrs. MacKenzie in her own large yard.

After dinner, she was curled up in an easy chair by the fireplace with a book when Calvin appeared before her.

"Need new boots, Mommy," he said in a matter of fact tone.

Ella looked down at his feet and saw that he had dug his hiking boots out of the closet and tried them on. "Your feet are growing," she observed aloud. Her voice held a hint of concern.

"My feet are hurtin'," he exclaimed.

Ella knew she couldn't afford to buy him new hiking boots — they just weren't a necessity. But looking into Calvin's face, she could see that to him they were. Especially now that he had a "job" as a guide.

"You're wearing your cereal aisle face, Mommy."

She stopped chewing her bottom lip and smiled instead. "I'll take a look around town on my lunch hour tomorrow for a pair," she told him, not wanting to ruin such a nice day with a tantrum. Perhaps she might find something on sale, she hoped, as Calvin beamed at her like she was a super hero and then limped away in his tight boots.

At lunch on Monday, Ella was somewhat relieved that she had a real excuse to use if Cate or Sarah asked her to go out with them. Although another problem presented itself as she roamed store after store and came away empty handed. It was the beginning of tourist season which, unfortunately for the residents of Caverly, meant the prices of everything had skyrocketed. The smart townspeople had done their shopping early, but Ella hadn't expected to be looking for hiking boots the second week of July. She returned to work worried about disappointing Calvin tonight, and cringed when five o'clock came and it was time to close up for the night.

Calvin was anxiously awaiting her arrival when she pulled up to Mrs. MacKenzie's house.

He didn't wait for her to even say hello before he asked what his new boots looked like.

"I'm sorry, babe. I couldn't find anything in your size, your feet have grown so much." Ella hated telling the lie, but she wanted to let him down gently. When she witnessed the sadness on his face she couldn't help but offer him a bit of hope. "I'll go back out again tomorrow and look, okay?"

"All right," he agreed grudgingly.

Ella thanked Mrs. MacKenzie and hurried Calvin into the car.

After dinner that night, she sat him down in the living room to prepare him for a let down over the boots. She wanted to do it when they were alone in case it got loud.

"It's very late in the season to be looking for hiking boots, and I might not be able to find any for you," she began.

"The season is just startin'."

"I know that, sweetie, but the stores don't work that way. If you want something for summer, the time to buy it is before the summer actually begins."

"You mean like in the spring?"

"Yes. Or sometimes even earlier."

"That's dumb," Calvin scoffed.

"I know it seems silly to you, but unfortunately, that's how stores work. And it is most likely that I won't find what you want. There isn't as much to choose from because everyone else has done their shopping early."

"And they didn't leave any for me?" he asked.

"No, sweetheart. They didn't leave any for you," Ella told him gently. She could have cried over the way he walked away from her with his head hanging low in defeat. She heard the click of his bedroom door and knew that he had gone off to be alone. It could have been much worse, she reasoned. Instead of taking it so bravely, he could have screamed and bawled or thrown himself down on the floor in a hysterical fit. But as she listened to him crying softly through his door, she knew she would have preferred the tantrum.

At work the next day, Ella asked Sarah if she would mind covering for her in case she happened to return a little late from lunch. She wanted to head over to the next town, which was about fifteen miles away. As she hopped into her car she tried not to think about what it was she intended to do. Instead, she would think about the look of joy on Calvin's face when she handed him new boots tonight. That was, if she was successful at pawning her necklace. She hated to do it because it had been a gift from Joe for her twenty-third birthday. She had other necklaces and pieces of jewelry from Joe, so selling one of them to buy something special for their son would be worth it, she assured herself.

The man behind the counter offered her twenty-five dollars. It was a fraction of the necklace's value, but as she looked into the man's business-like face she knew he would go no higher. Ella recalled she'd seen a pair of boots Calvin's size for about that same amount. She took the money the man offered, remembering how large the sum of twenty-five dollars had seemed to her yesterday. She hurried back into Caverly, picked up the boots, and managed to get back to work being only ten minutes late.

She wasn't hesitant about picking up her son after work that evening. In fact, she couldn't wait for five o'clock to roll around. As she pulled up in front of Mrs. MacKenzie's house she could see Calvin standing at the front door. His head was still hanging low, and Ella guessed he probably hadn't raised it up all day. She got out of the car and walked toward him, holding the box, in which lay his boots, in her hands. She couldn't wait to give them to him, and had decided on the way there to let him have them now.

45

Calvin lifted his head as she approached the door, and spotted the box she held. The closer she got, the more curious he became, until finally, he could no longer contain his interest and pushed open the door.

"What's that box for, Mommy?" he asked, stepping outside, his gaze entirely focused on it.

Mrs. MacKenzie, who had also been watching from the door, came outside to greet her. Ella spared her only a quick "Hello." All her attention was focused on the look of excitement on Calvin's face. She knelt down before him and passed him the box.

Calvin hesitated only a second before he lifted the lid and peered within.

"There was something left for you after all, sweet pea," she whispered as Calvin jumped into her arms and hugged her fiercely.

He insisted on wearing the boots home. He then wore them through dinner, and all evening as well. Ella begged him to take them off for bed and he finally relented, after telling her that he'd broken them in well enough. When she fell into bed, exhausted from the long day, she smiled as she recalled the joy on Calvin's face when she'd surprised him. And then she cried. Never would she let on to him just how much the boots had really cost her.

The rest of the week flashed by in a blur for Ella, and all too soon, Saturday had arrived. She stood with Calvin, early in the morning, before the cereal aisle at the grocery store. Surprisingly, he gave her no complaint when she put healthy, inexpensive cereal into the cart. This time, it was the fruit section that gave her trouble.

"Want grapes for lunch, Mommy," he announced, standing before her straight and tall in his new boots. He'd worn them every day since she'd given them to him.

Ella balked when she saw the price and looked at Calvin with trepidation. There was no way she could afford to buy grapes if she were to buy the rest of the fruit she needed for the week.

Then a thought came to her. "Calvin, Gabriel will probably have a nice lunch already packed up for us when we get there." *No doubt about it*, she thought bitterly, trying to keep the ire from her voice. "If we pack a lunch too, his feelings may be hurt." Ella looked at Calvin anxiously as she spoke, assessing his reaction to her words. She knew she allowed her son too much control over situations, especially in public, for fear of his tantrums. She'd never wanted to be an overindulgent parent, and in reality, she couldn't afford to be. Being held captive to his outbursts was the price she paid for trying to compensate for the fact that his father was gone. Taking back the reins now was proving to be difficult. Joe had always been the firm one, and now that it fell to her, she felt incapable of the task.

He appeared thoughtful for a moment, and even placed a finger to his chin in contemplation.

"Think he'll remember to pack the grapes?"

Ella silently begged God in that moment that Gabriel wouldn't forget. "I'm sure he will."

"Okay, then I guess we don't need to get 'em."

She breathed a sigh of relief, and when she put the groceries into the trunk ten minutes later, she realized this was the first time in months Calvin hadn't had a tantrum in the store.

At ten o'clock sharp, according to Calvin's watch, Ella was knocking on the door of her uncle's cottage. Gabriel answered almost immediately, and she could see that he was all ready to go. He had on rugged hiking boots of his own, and wore blue jeans and a light blue T-shirt. His brown hair lay damp around his shoulders from the shower, and she guessed he must have just shaved because he smelled strongly of cologne.

"Hi, there. Come on in," he invited them charmingly.

"The bugs are going to love you," Ella told him as she passed by.

"Yeah, you smell kinda funny," Calvin observed, sniffing dramatically.

Ella was embarrassed. "Calvin, what have I told you about saying things like that?"

Gabriel laughed before he could answer. "It's okay, I guess I did splash it on a little thick. I haven't been up north in a while, and I'd forgotten how the bugs love this stuff. Make yourselves at home," he offered as he strode toward the bathroom.

Ella knew he was going to try to wash off some of the cologne, but she figured it wouldn't make much of a difference—the damage was already done. The mosquitoes became quite overzealous when you got into the thick of the forest. The only way to keep them off was to use a ton of bug repellent, but even that wouldn't keep you safe if you smelled really good to them. And Ella had to admit, if only to herself, that Gabriel smelled delicious.

She was looking out the large front window when he came out of the bathroom. He walked over and bent down before Calvin.

"Better?" he asked, while Calvin leaned toward him and sniffed.

"I can still smell ya, but it's better."

"I'm sure you'll be fine," Ella interjected, trying to compensate for her son's rudeness.

Gabriel stood back up and looked at his watch. "Well, time's a wasting. Shall we go?"

"Yeah, time's a wastin'," Calvin agreed, looking at his own watch. He then dug his hand into the pocket of his jeans and pulled out a wrinkled paper. "My map," he told Gabriel when he saw him glance at it. As Ella struggled to overcome her humiliation at having Gabriel see Calvin wearing the watch from the cereal box, he then declared, "All we need now are the grapes and we can go."

Ten minutes later the canoe was cutting smoothly over the lake with its three occupants.

Ella dipped her paddle into the water mechanically while she concentrated on her thoughts. She had to say something to Gabriel about the cereal he had stashed in her trunk, but she wasn't sure how to broach the subject without completely shaming herself. Should she begin with "You really shouldn't have," or should she say something along the lines of "Who do you think you are?" Either way, it had to be done, she just needed to come up with the right words because she couldn't ignore the matter any longer. Especially with Calvin continuously flashing that watch around.

They pulled up before the rock face and Ella climbed out and tied off the rope. She hadn't spoken a word to Gabriel since he'd passed the picnic basket into her hands from the dock. Then she'd only mumbled "Thanks" and turned her flushed face away from him. Calvin had spared her from making polite conversation in the canoe while he explained in great detail to Gabriel the finer points of his detailed map.

When they all climbed onto the rock face, Calvin wasted no time in taking up the lead. Holding his map in his hands, he led them over to the trail, and as he began walking along he instructed them to "Keep close." Thankfully, the mosquitoes didn't seem too bad at all.

Ella couldn't take the silence between her and Gabriel any longer. They walked along behind Calvin, practically side by side, but she felt as though he were miles away from her.

When she caught a glimpse of his face, it occurred to her that she wasn't the only one with a lot on her mind. Gabriel's mouth was drawn in a grim line, and when she ventured to breach the subject of the watch, he turned to her suddenly.

"I'm sorry, did you say something?" he asked.

"Ah, yes. I said your name."

"Oh. What is it, Ella?"

His attention was now totally focused on her, and she suddenly felt unsure of her choice of words. "I...I wanted to talk to you about the other day, at the grocery store."

Gabriel appeared to understand what she was getting at right away. He lowered his gaze to the ground, concentrating on the trail they followed. "I shouldn't have done it. I realized that after I put the cereal in your trunk and watched you drive away. But by that time, it was too late."

Ella breathed a sigh of relief over his admission of error. She'd been afraid he might get defensive over his actions. Before she could say anything, he spoke again, though his face was now raised, his eyes focused on hers.

"I'm sorry. You have every right to decide what you buy for your son. I shouldn't have overstepped your decision. I'm afraid instead of helping I've made matters worse, because Calvin may expect you to give in to his demands now."

She thought about the boots she'd just bought for him. Gabriel was correct with his assessment. She'd given in instead of standing her ground. Perhaps she'd missed an important opportunity to teach Calvin a lesson. He had to learn that when she said no, she meant it.

"We all make mistakes, Gabriel. Lord knows I've lost count of how many I've made. Your heart was in the right place. I only brought it up because I wanted to make certain you understood my position. I can't possibly give Calvin everything he asks for, nor would I want to."

"You're a good mother, Ella. And you're right."

She looked at her son, who was proudly walking on ahead of them, leading the way. She felt undeserving of the compliment, thinking of all the things she'd done wrong with Calvin, but she couldn't deny she had enjoyed hearing it.

"So, what's a big-time author like you doing in the drab little town of Caverly?" she asked teasingly, changing the topic.

His face immediately became tense again, and Ella feared she'd spoken out of turn. It wasn't any of her business what he was doing here, and she sunk her teeth into her bottom lip, wishing suddenly that she could take back her words.

He took a moment to respond to the question. "I guess you could say I'm hiding out."

"Hiding from what?" Ella asked, wondering what a man

who was as famous and successful as he was possibly had to hide from. All his many fans perhaps? He did say he'd been followed before.

"I couldn't take living in the shadow of my former accomplishments any longer."

"What do you mean, Gabriel? All of your novels were bestsellers."

"All except the last one," he reminded her. "I think I've lost it."

"Lost what?"

"My creativity," he admitted in a desolate tone. "It's gone."

Chapter Four

"Gabriel, you know that writer's block isn't uncommon — it'll pass," Ella told him gently.

He ran his hand through his hair in frustration. "I know. I keep telling myself the same thing. It's not as though it hasn't happened to me before, but this time it's different."

"How so?"

"It's like I'm all tapped out of ideas or something. Like the well has run dry."

Ella could hear the strain in his voice. She knew all too well how it felt when stress overtook you and all you could dwell on was your failure. "When I'm feeling overwhelmed, I think of something else, anything else, to get my mind off what it is that's making me upset. If you can find a way to put it aside, you can approach it later."

"That's what I was hoping to do by coming up here. I thought if I got out of the city I could leave the pressure behind, but that doesn't seem to be the case. It's like I brought it up here with me and I can't get away from it."

"We're turning off here," Calvin yelled back at them. "Be sure to keep close."

Ella and Gabriel looked at Calvin, then at each other and suddenly burst into laughter.

"You know, your boy there is a great distraction," Gabriel said, after they quieted down.

"He is, isn't he?" Ella agreed.

"This is exactly what I needed today," he said, the tension draining from his voice, his mouth no longer drawn tightly in a frown. His step picked up a pace, as though he'd cast off a heavy burden.

"We'll be there in a while. I can't wait for you to see Bethower Lake," she told him, relieved he had finally begun to relax. She didn't know why it meant so much to her that Gabriel should enjoy today, when only a week ago she'd resented his interference in her and Calvin's life. But now, after hearing him talk about his own feelings of inadequacy, it somehow made him seem vulnerable to her. No longer did it feel as though he were the wildly successful author, and she the impoverished widow. The distance between them had magically shrunk with his confession.

When they pushed aside the bushes and stepped out onto a slight clearing before the lake, Calvin was already there waiting for them. Though only arriving moments before, he'd already stretched out on the smooth rock and crossed his ankles before him, as though he'd been there all day.

"What took ya so long?" he teased.

"Wow," Gabriel exclaimed, gazing at their surroundings in wonder.

Ella remembered how Bethower had looked the first time she'd seen it. Like finding an oasis in the desert, its beauty had amazed her too. She smiled at the look of delight on Gabriel's face.

"It's great, isn't it?"

He nodded his head in agreement. "No one has a cottage on this lake?"

"Not that we've ever seen. I have portaged up here a couple of times to take a peek around some of those bays." She pointed to the far right side of the small lake.

"That must have been fantastic to go out on the water."

"It was."

"Is this still crown land then?"

"Yes. Owned by the government, for now. They've sold off property around the other side of Loon Lake, which was once crown land, so I can't say for sure that this might not be sold off as well."

"It seems a shame."

"Can we eat some of those grapes now?" Calvin yelled over at them.

Gabriel had placed the picnic basket down beside Calvin before walking over to the edge of the water. Ella still held the blanket she had taken from him awhile back on the trail.

"Good idea, I'm starved." Gabriel briskly rubbed his hands together while he walked over and crouched down before the picnic basket. Calvin got up to help Ella lay the blanket out, and then waited for Gabriel to pass the food around.

The blanket was soon overflowing with lunchmeat and cheese and a fresh bread stick. Ella had to suppress a laugh when she saw the euphoric look on Calvin's face when he spied the apple pie and the can of whipped cream. Gabriel had remembered how much Calvin liked drinking from the plastic wine cups, so he'd included those, along with a carton of chocolate milk. To her relief, he'd also brought a big bunch of grapes.

When lunch was finished and cleared away, Gabriel showed Calvin how to skip stones across the surface of the water. After several tries he finally succeeded with making a rock skip once.

"It's a start," Gabriel told him, as he made his own rock skip an astonishing six times.

"I can show you how to make a sap boat," Calvin boasted.

"A sap boat?"

"Yeah, follow me." He picked up a little stick and then searched around for another and passed it to Gabriel. He rushed into the forest and ran up to one of the many balsam trees.

"Just poke your stick into these bubbles, but be careful 'cause it squirts sometimes."

Gabriel watched as Calvin poked at the tree, then smeared the sap onto the end of his stick.

He copied Calvin's actions, being careful not to get squirted. They covered the ends of their sticks with sap until they were dripping, and then Calvin rushed back to the edge of the water with a curious Gabriel right behind him.

"Now, throw it in," Calvin instructed.

"After all that you just want me to throw it away?"

As Calvin dropped his stick into the water, Ella came over to watch. She smiled at Gabriel, who had still refused to toss his in. His eyes were focused on Calvin's stick and the sap, which had turned into a beautiful colored rainbow which flowed out across the surface of the water and moved the stick forward.

"It looks the way gasoline does when it spills into water," Gabriel said in wonder. He then dropped his own stick into the lake, and watched it light up with color and propel itself up beside Calvin's.

"It's a boat," Calvin told him.

"So it is," Gabriel agreed, watching their sticks float away.

The afternoon sun shone down through the tall trees, spearing the trail with flashes of bright light. Calvin's boots crunched dead leaves that carpeted the forest floor while he strode on ahead of the pair, who were talking not far behind. Gabriel was regaling Ella with his adventures on a London trip he'd taken years ago, exploring old castles for research on a book he'd been working on.

"I've always wanted to go to London, all of Britain really. The history there fascinates me," Ella told him.

"It is incredible, I have to say."

"I'm embarrassed to tell you I have never left the country. Actually, that's not quite true. I once crossed the border with Joe when we went to Niagara Falls on our honeymoon. We saw the falls from the Canadian side and then came right back."

Gabriel laughed, and when Ella flushed over her admission, he told her that he had never been to Niagara Falls. Then it was Ella's turn to laugh.

"It's true," he confessed.

"Well, you must go then. It's spectacular. I want to take

Calvin there some day."

Returning to the cottage, Ella was amazed when Calvin told her his watch read two-zero-five.

She couldn't believe that it was after two o'clock. Time had slipped away while she and Gabriel had strolled along following Calvin, who had again taken up the lead with his map in hand.

They had talked all the way back along the trail, and even as they crossed over the lake in the canoe. He'd told her about his travels to different countries, and how he'd found inspiration for his stories in the beauty and the intrigue of the places he'd explored and the people he'd met.

He'd gone into detail about his writing, and Ella had been pleased he could talk about it now without appearing tense. She'd found his tales captivating, and she felt she could listen to him speak of them all day. Then he had turned the conversation to her life and she'd grown silent, not knowing what to say. Her life in comparison with his seemed so unexciting. But he had drawn her out, like a timid rabbit from its hollow. Since she kept insisting there was nothing to tell, he had asked her questions, especially about Calvin. And what mother can refuse to boast about her child? She had found that she could easily bring herself to talk about her son.

All too soon they had arrived back at the cottage and they were bidding each other a reluctant goodbye. Later, when she and Calvin pulled into the driveway of their home, she noticed a small blue car parked there that she didn't recognize.

"Who is it, Mommy?" A sleepy Calvin asked her as she took his hand and led him to the house.

"I'm not sure, honey," Ella replied, genuinely puzzled.

She didn't see anyone around, but perhaps her visitor had gone into the backyard to await her arrival.

They went in the front door and Ella walked into the kitchen to look out back to see if anyone was there. She spotted two young women sitting at the picnic table. One had shoulder length light brown hair, and the other, short dark brown curls. It took her just a moment to realize they were Jen and Katherine.

Ella quickly opened the door and called out while she rushed over to greet them. "I hardly recognized you, Jen, with your short hair." She hugged them both tightly to her, and they were soon joined by Calvin.

"What's all the yelling about?" he demanded, then laid eyes on the girls and hollered out his own welcome. "You came! You came! Mommy said you might."

Jen bent down to ruffle Calvin's hair. "Hey squirt."

Katherine knelt down and gave him a tight squeeze, which Calvin immediately struggled out of. "We're here to visit for a while. Is that all right with you, buddy?"

"Sure," Calvin replied. "You can't stay at your cottage though, cause it's rented to Mister Gab-real. He's nice. Mommy and I spend lots of time with him."

Ella blushed bright red as her cousins turned their curious glances on her after hearing Calvin's words.

"Really?" Jen drawled. "Tell us all about this Mister Gab-real, Calvin."

"We don't know him all that well, Jen," Ella offered lamely.

"But Mommy, you should know him well by now, 'cause you guys talked all the way back from Bethower Lake."

Julie Parker

"You don't say?" Katherine declared.

"Calvin, that's quite enough explaining, young man. Why don't you run along inside now?" Ella suggested in a tone that allowed no discussion.

"Okay, okay," Calvin sulked, then turned and walked back inside the house.

"We'll talk later, kiddo," Jen called after him, giving her sister a knowing wink.

Ella made up a pot of tea after dinner and they sat outside on the patio, all talking at once. "I can't believe so much has happened in your lives in just one year," she exclaimed after listening to the girls bring her up to date. She wasn't surprised when Jen admitted she'd sprained her ankle jumping from a plane a month ago.

"She's lucky that's all that got hurt considering the outlandish things Nicky got her to try," Katherine snapped, her disapproval of the man evident.

"Who's Nicky?" Ella asked.

"He was my boyfriend. He's not anymore," Jen said.

Her expression was hard to read, and Ella wasn't sure if she should continue with the questions or let it be. She decided to change the subject. "So tell me, did you two know that Uncle Lionel had rented the cottage to Gabriel Stolks?"

The girls exchanged a quick look before Jen answered her question. "Dad told us that he'd rented it to a writer, but he didn't elaborate on who it was."

"I take it he's the Mister Gab-real Calvin was talking about?" Katherine asked.

"Yes," Ella replied feeling a familiar blush upon her face once again. "Calvin's quite taken with him."

"It sounds like you're quite taken with him too," Jen observed.

"No, it's not like that, really. You know I work at the library, and of course I know who he is. I just found him interesting to talk to, that's all."

"So, how did it go when you two met?" Katherine asked.

Ella gave her cousin a piercing look. "Did your father tell you that he sent me over to the cottage with every intention of having us run into each other?"

Katherine ducked her guilt-ridden face. "I admit, I did know. We both knew," she confessed, nodding in Jen's direction.

"It wasn't our idea, though," Jen told her.

"Your dad doesn't need any help coming up with ideas of how to snag me a date—he does well enough on his own."

"It's the romantic in him. He and Mom are still so crazy in love, and he just thinks that everyone should feel that way," Katherine explained.

"I know," Ella sighed.

Though she hadn't intended to, she wound up telling her cousins the story about the silly misunderstanding between her and Gabriel when they had met at the cottage. She explained how they had first run into each other at the grocery store. That they had exchanged pleasantries but not names, and she hadn't known at that time what he was doing in Caverly. She left out the part about her and Calvin having a tug-a-war over a box of cereal that she couldn't afford. She also left out the part about her falling over in the aisle in front of Gabriel, and how he had sneaked the cereal into her trunk. The girls howled with laughter when she told them

61

how Calvin had offered to be Gabriel's guide, and that he had even brought along his very own map for today's adventure. And then, in the midst of all the laughter, Jen suddenly broke into tears.

Ella was shocked by her cousin's sudden change in emotions. "What is it Jen, what's wrong?" she asked, reaching out to hold her cousin's hand in comfort.

Katherine rolled her eyes over the show her sister was putting on. "Don't mind her. She'll only get this way every hour or so. It's been going on all week."

"I can't help it," Jen whined pitifully. "I miss Nicky."

~*~

Monday morning at work, Ella told Cate and Sarah about the unexpected arrival of her two cousins. "I was hoping to take my vacation earlier if that's all right with you guys."

The library was empty for the moment, and Ella felt it would be a good time to call the girls over to the information desk where she was sitting so she could talk to them. Her cousins were at her house entertaining Calvin for her, insisting they look after him while she went to work.

She had told Mrs. Mackenzie at church yesterday that she wouldn't need her to watch him for a while. It had worked out pretty good, Ella thought, since the money she saved on babysitting could now be spent on extra expenses, like groceries, while Jen and Katherine were in town. She did have two weeks of paid vacation coming to her though, and she had yet to pick out a date.

She usually waited until her aunt and uncle came up north for their vacation, and then she would book time off to be with them.

"I thought your uncle had rented out the cottage for the summer," Cate said.

"He did. I had suggested to him that it'd be good for the girls to come down and stay with me, though. Calvin adores them, and I really didn't want the summer to pass without seeing them," Ella explained.

"I think it's great," Sarah told her. "If you want to take your vacation now, it's fine with me."

"Me too," Cate agreed. "I don't want to take any time off this summer."

"You don't?" Ella asked, although she wasn't very surprised. Most people wanted a summer vacation so they could leave the bustle of the city behind. But since they already lived up north, there wasn't the desperate need in them to escape.

"No, I wanted to get away in the late fall instead. I've been saving up to go somewhere warm."

"Hey, how about all of us get together one night?" Sarah suggested.

Oh, no, here we go again, Ella worried. "I don't know," she hesitated, the wheels frantically spinning in her mind to come up with an excuse. "I only have Mrs. Mackenzie for a sitter, and I would have to bring Calvin to her house because she hates to drive at night. And then if we were late he'd have to sleep there. I don't feel very comfortable leaving him. He's never spent the night away from home, so I think he would probably put up quite a fuss."

"You really need to find another sitter, Ella, for the evenings. Someone who could come to your house. That way you could start going out with us the odd Friday night like you used to."

"Joe used to watch him on those nights," Ella said despondently.

"Oh, Ella. I'm sorry," Sarah said. "I didn't mean to upset you. I just miss you going out with us; we used to have fun."

"I know," Ella said. "It's okay, you didn't upset me. Actually, you're right, I really should find a sitter for evenings." *If only I could afford to pay for one*, she silently added.

~*~

"Mommy, what's all this weird stuff?" Calvin asked, looking down at his plate.

Ella smiled tightly at him while she struggled to keep her temper. She'd worked hard on this dish, and didn't appreciate the rude comment or the look of distaste on Calvin's face. "It's called chicken pot pie."

"Doesn't look like no pie. Pie has apples or blueberries in it, not all these gross things."

"That's chicken and vegetables in a creamy sauce."

"It's good, Calvin," Jen told him while she dug into her own.

"Yes, it's very tasty," Katherine agreed.

Feeling somewhat mollified, Ella was pleased with the praise over her efforts. It hadn't been easy the past couple of days to come up with meals for everyone. This recipe was the newest creation. Last night she'd made a stir-fry including some of her string beans from the garden, which had helped to stretch it a bit. Her cousins helped out by washing all of the dishes after each meal and watching Calvin for her while she cooked. Unfortunately, it had been a bit of a struggle to feed an extra two adults with what she had in the cupboard. She would have run to the grocery store for more supplies, but she couldn't afford to shop again so soon.

"What's this on the top?" Calvin asked, poking his fork into his dinner.

"It's stuffing," Ella said.

"Stuffing is supposed to be in a turkey," he told her, his tone lofty.

"Well, this time it's serving as the top of the chicken pie."

Calvin scooped up a tiny piece on his fork and made a show of eating it. The face he made after placing it in his mouth could only be described as one of horror. He did attempt to chew it—with large exaggerated bites—then swallowed it down, resembling a boa constrictor with a large cow stuck in its throat. He then drank all of his milk to make sure the offending piece of stuffing was washed down entirely. "I tried it, and I don't like it," he stated.

"You're going to eat that," Ella insisted.

Calvin met her stare, engaging in a battle of wills. "Then you're gonna need a lot more milk."

Ella sighed and got up from the table to make him a peanut butter sandwich.

They sat outside around a bonfire after dinner, roasting marshmallows for dessert. Calvin's stick was over four feet long, keeping him well away from the flames, but Ella still kept a wary eye on him. As was his custom, he'd shove his marshmallow deep into the fire as soon as he stuck it on the end of his stick. He took great pleasure in watching it burst into flames, which he promptly blew out before sliding the sticky mass of ashes off and popping them into his eager mouth. Ella watched him eat, and wondered if there was anything she could cook that he would devour with such gusto.

"Nicky and I camped out together the long weekend in May," Jen suddenly announced.

"Here we go again," Katherine sighed, dropping her head into her hands.

"Where did you go?" Ella asked kindly, becoming familiar with Jen's need to rehash her glory days with her old boyfriend. In the first few months after Joe's death she had wanted to talk about him all the time, going on and on about things they'd done together to anyone who would listen. She felt she needed to speak of him, to say his name. It had almost kept him alive for her in a way. If she didn't talk about him, she feared people might forget him. That *she* might forget him. The most frightening day was when she couldn't remember how his voice had sounded, and then his face began to fade from her memory.

"We went all the way up to Algonquin Park," Jen stated, interrupting her thoughts.

"That's a long way." Ella pretended to be impressed. She could just imagine how her aunt and uncle must have felt about their daughter's little excursion, though.

Jen laughed all of a sudden as she remembered something funny. "We drove all the way up there and discovered we'd forgotten our tent."

Ignoring Katherine's glare, Ella asked her what they'd done.

"Well, it was too late to go back for it, so we decided to hike to our campsite anyway. We walked for almost an hour until we came upon a clearing by a sparkling stream. You should have seen it, Ella; it was picture perfect."

66

"Yeah, and she's got the pictures to prove it — stacks of 'em."

Jen stuck her tongue out at her sister, then continued. "Being such an awesome woodsman, Nicky gathered a bunch of tall branches and made a lean-to for our shelter. It was perfect."

"Isn't that the weekend you got poison ivy?" Katherine reminded her.

Jen ignored her. Katherine stuck her finger down her throat and pretended to gag.

"We put a layer of pine branches down on the floor, and when we spread out our sleeping bags we had a cozy bed for the night."

"Made a shelter, did he? Sounds like a resourceful young man," Ella stated.

"Young. Ha! That's a laugh," Katherine said.

Seeing Ella's confused look, Jen attempted to explain. "That was the problem, you see. Nicky is almost thirty."

Chapter Five

In the morning, Katherine located Ella in the kitchen preparing breakfast. She walked over and tapped her gently on the shoulder. When Ella turned, Katherine passed two one hundred dollars bills into her hand.

"What's this for?" Ella asked, staring at the money.

"Dad said to give it to you so Jen and I don't eat you out of house and home." Ella tried to pass it back to Katherine, but she clasped her hands behind her back, refusing to accept it. "Dad insisted. Please take it — I'm sorry I forgot to give it to you sooner. I only remembered this morning."

"You girls are not going to eat that much," Ella insisted.

"You haven't seen how much Jen can put away lately. Don't let her scrawny little body fool you."

"I heard that!" Jen stated in mock outrage as she entered the kitchen. "What's for breakfast? I'll eat anything as long as Katherine didn't cook it."

Ella had to resist the urge to say "Touché" when she saw

the look on Katherine's face.

~*~

"Don't get too close to the edge!" Ella hollered, as Calvin ran up the side of a rock-face to gaze over the hill. They had driven up to Eagle's Landing, the largest hill in Caverly, and then climbed by foot over the rolling trails toward the edge to behold the town below. Off in the distance they viewed the best of what the northern country had to offer. Their eyes were met by lush green trees, crystal blue lakes that dotted the landscape, and rolling hills as far as the eye could see.

The cliff they stood upon was steep and treacherous, and the bottom was fittingly home to one of the town's cemeteries. The first time she and Joe had come up here together, Ella recalled he had jokingly told her if she happened to fall from this spot there'd be no need to bury her, because she'd hit the ground so hard and fast she'd do the job herself. It had been comical at the time, but now, as she watched her son dancing dangerously close to the cliff's edge, overlooking the cemetery where his father now lay, Ella didn't think the jest was quite so amusing anymore.

"I see our house, Mommy."

Ella stepped up beside Calvin on the rock to dutifully peer into the distance where he pointed, trying to spot their house.

"Do you see it? Do you, Mommy?"

"Yes, I think so," she exclaimed.

"And I see Loon Lake." Katherine pointed in another direction.

"Oh, is that Gabriel Stolks I see out in the boat?" Jen teased.

"Maybe he's gonna try out the map I left him," Calvin said, staring hard into the thick forest, attempting to spot him.

"Jen's just being silly, Calvin. She can't see Gabriel from way up here," Ella told him.

"I'm getting hungry, and my watch says it's time for lunch, Mommy," Calvin said, tapping his watch.

Before Ella had a chance to distract him, Katherine bent down to admire Calvin's watch.

"Very good," she told him, noting the time said twelve o'clock.

Calvin smiled over the praise and then opened his mouth to talk more about his new talent.

"I learned to tell time with this new watch Mommy got me. It's from the grocery store, and it was in a box of cereal. I was kinda surprised Mommy got it for me seein' as how we had a tug-a-war in the aisle over it, then she fell over right in front of —"

"Calvin!" Ella interrupted. "You don't need to go into detail, young man," she chastised, her face flaming red with embarrassment.

"A tug-a-war, eh?" Jen laughed. Calvin laughed too, encouraged by the attention he was generating.

Ella looked at him and didn't see her son in that moment, but a dog with a bone who was getting ready to run with it. She had to put a stop to this right away, before Calvin spilled the beans about what had happened that day. If he kept talking he might let it slip that she couldn't afford the cereal. He then might say something about not buying the grapes. It wouldn't take too many of these little slips before her cousins figured out she was broke.

"It was a sugar cereal, and we'd already decided we were going to get cookies. Too many sweets aren't good for him," she explained, hoping they bought it.

"But Mommy, you did get me cookies."

"You must have been a very good boy to get two treats then," Katherine told him.

"How about we eat lunch in town today?" Ella suggested, anxiously hoping to stop Calvin from saying anything more about the grocery store. She had one of the hundred dollar bills that Katherine had given her in her purse, and she would use some of it to treat them all to lunch. Besides, she needed a distraction before Calvin told how she'd fallen flat on her face in the aisle in front of Gabriel.

"I thought we couldn't eat lunch in town no more, Mommy."

"No, no, honey, you misunderstood," she said quickly. "I told you that I enjoy eating at home more than eating out."

"I'm the same way," Katherine said. "It's okay to go out once in a while, but I enjoy home cooking much more."

"As long as you're not the one who's doing the cooking," Jen said.

"My cooking isn't that bad," Katherine insisted.

While the two of them argued, Ella took the opportunity to hurry Calvin back along the trail toward the car. When she unlocked the door for him and helped him into his car seat, she breathed a sigh of relief. The topic of the watch and the cereal had mercifully been forgotten, and she was actually looking forward to eating out, considering it had been a while since she'd indulged in that luxury.

They ate at a little family restaurant in town called Mom's, and Ella let Calvin order whatever he liked from the menu. He settled for a burger with fries and a big chocolate milkshake. Her cousins ordered the same, but Ella decided on a grilled cheese sandwich and a cola. All of a sudden she wasn't feeling very hungry — even the sight of the juicy burgers or the crispy fries arriving at their table failed to tempt her. Though spending money on lunch put a guilty knot in her stomach, it was worth it, she decided, just to see Calvin's face when his milkshake in a tall glass was placed before him, and his eyes lit up like it was Christmas. He ate with the same gusto he'd shown when devouring the marshmallows, but was still only able to finish half of his burger. Ella asked to have it wrapped up to bring home, knowing he would probably want to finish it for dinner when he got a look at the meatloaf she planned to serve tonight.

The phone rang just as she was setting out dessert after dinner, and Ella was glad for the interruption. Jen had seen the Jell-O mold she'd made for dessert, and it had reminded her of another moment shared with Nicky.

It was Gabriel on the phone, and he was attempting to tell her about a problem he was having.

"The pump keeps coming on, and I can't seem to figure out why."

Ella thought for a moment. "It could be there's a leak somewhere that you're unaware of," she said. "Have you checked underneath the cottage?"

"I have, but I didn't see any water."

"It may need to be primed again."

"Okay, just tell me what to do and I'll give it a try," he said with little enthusiasm.

She couldn't help but laugh. "I think you'd better leave this one to me, Gabriel. I'll be right up, okay?"

"I hate to drag you out so late, especially with Calvin."

"My cousins are in town visiting. I'll leave Calvin at home with them," she told him.

"Oh, that's great. Thanks a lot. I'll see you soon then."

Ella hung up the phone and called Katherine over to her. "I need to go to the cottage to take a look at the pump, Gabriel said it won't shut off. Would you mind watching Calvin for me?"

"No, of course not," Katherine told her. "Take all the time you need," she added with a wink.

Katherine asked Calvin to grab a board game to play, and he was so excited over the match he hardly spared Ella a goodbye when she kissed him and said she was going out for a while.

When she arrived at the cottage, Gabriel was on the back porch waiting for her. "I can't thank you enough for this, Ella. I felt bad calling you so late, but I didn't think I should wait. When the pump didn't turn off, I kind of panicked and pulled the main switch to shut everything down."

"You were right to call, and you did the right thing turning off the power," she reassured him. "Don't worry about the time; I'm on vacation for the next couple of weeks."

Ella headed around to the side of the cottage and crawled underneath to get a look at the pump. Gabriel crouched down and watched, but didn't attempt to crawl over to join her. She spared him a glance, and thought with his great size he probably would have a difficult time fitting into the low space.

73

After a few moments of checking the system, Ella announced she had discovered the problem. "It's as I thought, it needs to be primed again."

"Can I help?" Gabriel asked, swatting a mosquito.

"Yes. There should be a bucket in the bedroom with the electrical panel. Can you grab it and fill it up in the lake, please? Oh, and push the power switch back up."

"Okay," he said, quickly standing up to head inside.

He returned a few minutes later and placed the bucket underneath the cottage. She reached for the water and began to slowly pour it into the line of the pump. It took almost fifteen minutes before she finally heard the pump begin to hum and she knew it was working correctly.

She crawled out and Gabriel helped her to her feet. Her legs were cramped and sore, and she leaned against the cottage for a moment. "It's working now," she told him.

He offered her his arm and she gratefully placed her hand on his elbow. "How long have you known how to do that?" he asked, as he slowly led her around the cottage.

"Oh, it's easy once you get the hang of it. My uncle showed me what to do when I was a teenager, in case I ever came up on my own."

"That makes sense. I guess it'd be a pretty long drive for him to come up here to help you if you had a problem with it." He stopped at the back of the cottage and Ella moved away from him.

Gabriel looked uncomfortable for a moment, and when she eyed him curiously he told her what he was thinking. "Would it be too much trouble for you to wait around until that thing shuts off?" he asked, referring to the pump which was still running.

Ella smiled over his embarrassment, knowing it must be hard for such a big, strong, independent man to ask a woman for help. "The pump is just filling up the holding tank," she explained. "It'll shut off in a few minutes. But I'll stay until it does, just to be sure it's working properly."

"Come in for coffee then?"

"That'd be great."

He stepped back to let her walk ahead of him. Once inside, she took a seat at the kitchen table while he filled the coffee pot with bottled water and switched it on. The silence grew awkward as he leaned against the counter, waiting for the pot to brew. Ella felt at a loss for words. The last time they'd been together, they'd talked so openly and she'd felt at ease. But now, after spending time apart, she suddenly felt self-conscious around him again.

"So, your cousins are in town?" he asked, breaking the silence.

"My Uncle Lionel's girls."

"Are they up for a vacation?"

"Yes. I had asked my uncle if they could spend some time with me. I must admit, I was a little upset when I'd discovered they had rented the cottage out. I really only get to see my family in the summer."

"I'm surprised your uncle would rent it then."

"Oh, I'm sure he had his reasons," Ella said dryly, knowing full well what his reasons were.

"So, you're on vacation now?"

"Yes, I am. I'm very lucky to work with a couple of great girls at the library. They're covering for me so I can spend time with Jen and Katherine, my cousins."

"I bet Calvin is enjoying the company."

Ella smiled. "He is," she agreed. "So how is *your* vacation going?"

Gabriel turned to grab a couple of mugs from the cupboard. "It's relaxing up here," he said, watching the coffee brew.

Ella detected a bit of tension in his voice, and knew he hadn't been able to put his worries aside completely. She got an idea, one that might help him forget about writing. "The jamboree is this weekend. How would you like to go with Calvin and me and my cousins?"

"Really?" he asked. "Are you certain you'd like to go?"

Ella sighed. She knew he was really thinking, *Are you now ready to go*? considering she hadn't been at the jamboree since Joe's death. "I think it'll be fun if we all go together."

"I'd like that. Thank you for the invitation." He poured the coffee and passed a mug over to her.

"The pump has turned off now," she told him, taking the steaming mug into her hands and nodding her thanks.

"Yeah. Let's just hope it works from now on so I won't have to bother you with any more house-calls."

Ella laughed lightly. "It's all right, I don't mind."

Gabriel suggested they take their coffee out onto the front deck and she agreed. They sat looking out toward the water and she felt a peaceful feeling settle over her. She sneaked a glance at Gabriel, and could tell by the slight smile on his face that he too was enjoying the moment. Small waves from the lake lapped against the shore while a soft breeze floated around them. Ella leaned back in her chair and closed her eyes, feeling suddenly drowsy despite the caffeine she sipped. Neither of them wanted to break the silence, both content to sit companionably side by side as the evening approached.

"Ouch!" Gabriel yelled suddenly, smacking at a mosquito on his thigh. The pest, narrowly escaping, was not deterred by the assault, but renewed its efforts toward finding that which it sought—the blood of man. A small bite was now the least of Gabriel's worries as his flailing sent his coffee spilling onto his chest. "Ow!" He jumped to his feet, and the mug fell to the deck and broke.

Ella placed her own mug down before leaping up to aid Gabriel. But she was too late, for he had already ripped the shirt from his massive chest and thrown it aside. He stood before her, gasping and slightly in shock from the spill, which had indeed been hot, but thankfully, not scalding. She grabbed his hand and pulled him down the stairway toward the water, which she entered after kicking off her shoes, and began to bathe his chest with the coolness of the lake. As her hands ran over his muscles, her thoughts began to turn from concern to desire.

She lifted her gaze and found his eyes glazed over—with what, she knew not, be it agony of his mishap or another pain entirely. Before she knew what was happening, he had lifted his hands and sunk them deeply into the thickness of her hair, and lowered his head to place his lips gently on hers.

His kiss was seeking, as though he silently asked her in that moment to join with him on this wild ride they had suddenly found themselves on. Then he groaned as if he were hurt, and though he'd not intended to break the moment, Ella became all too aware in that instant of what they were doing.

She ended the kiss, albeit with some reluctance, for she could not deny she had enjoyed their tryst, short as it had been. She backed away from him, and instead of meeting his gaze, she looked at his chest to determine if he had, in fact, been hurt. His skin was an angry pink, resembling a sunburn. She reached out and touched it tentatively, then looked up. "Does it hurt?"

"Not really," he replied.

His gaze was intense, and Ella backed farther away, fearing he might take her into his arms again to finish what he'd started. She bit her lip nervously, afraid she just might allow him to.

Her behavior toward him concerned her, considering she had made it clear in her mind a long time ago that she would never again become involved with a man. But it was obvious she had failed to make the matter clear to her body. She had let him draw her near and kiss her, and she had lost her resolve in that moment, becoming so caught up with the desperate longing he had awakened within her. When they had broken apart, she had a feeling of loneliness, an empty place longing to be filled.

She hoped he would let it go and pretend it had never happened, but it wasn't the case. When she came out of the water and began to walk toward the stairs, Gabriel caught up to her and placed himself in her path. Ella could not bring her eyes level with his; instead, she stared at the ground before her.

"I'm not going to say I'm sorry for what happened. It would be a lie, because I have wanted to kiss you since the first moment I saw you."

She tried to make her way around him, but he reached out and placed his hands on her shoulders.

"Let me by, Gabriel," she said. Her voice sounded defeated even to her, and she knew he wouldn't let her leave without acknowledging his admission.

"I know you're still mourning, but how much longer are you going to live your life denying your feelings?" he gently asked her.

"I have no feelings for you," she said cruelly, looking up at him and flashing a cold stare.

"I disagree."

She pulled out of his hold. "We kissed, Gabriel. That's all there was to it. Nothing more."

"I felt something, and I know you felt it too."

"Please, Gabriel," she begged, her voice breaking into a sob. "Let it go."

He pulled her against him, unmindful of his sore chest, and held her close in his strong arms.

Even as she weakly protested, his lips descended toward hers, his groan of victory drowning out the sounds of her denial. Ella finally succumbed to her desire and returned his kiss, matching his intensity. She ignored the sound of her wounded heart crying out for her to flee—before it was too late.

~*~

That night when Ella returned home and lay alone in her bed she felt afraid. This time it was not her lack of funds that kept her awake. No, it was much worse than that. For now it was herself she feared. The emotions coursing through her when she was with Gabriel had pushed her resolve to remain alone to the limits. But what could her foolish behavior hope to grant her? she asked herself, while tossing and turning in the darkness in frustration. After the summer ended, Gabriel would leave and she would again be alone. What could she possibly gain from their interlude but a wounded heart? Hours later, she finally drifted off into a restless sleep, dreaming of Joe, the look of disappointment he felt for her evident upon his face.

SEND ME AN ANGEL

Chapter Six

"You're up early this morning," Jen observed, walking across the kitchen, rubbing the sleep from her eyes.

Ella sat at the table with a cup of coffee, peering off into space. "Think so?"

Jen poured herself a cup and took a seat across from her. "I'm just a little surprised, because you came in pretty late last night."

"Oh. Did I? I didn't notice the time," she replied distractedly.

Jen looked hard at her. "Are you all right?"

"Sure. Just tired. I didn't sleep well."

Katherine entered the room at that moment and headed straight for the coffee. Soon the three of them were sitting around the table, all staring at each other.

"How did it go last night with Calvin?" Ella asked, wanting to head them off before they started asking about how her evening went.

"He was fine, just went to bed a little late."

That explained why it was eight-fifteen and he was still asleep, she thought.

"So, did you get the pump fixed?" Jen asked, a little smirk playing on her lips.

She could tell by the scrutiny on her cousins' faces that they were going to analyze every word she spoke. "Yes, it's running fine now."

"Did it take you long?"

"No, not really," she said carefully, knowing full well that Jen was baiting her.

"So then, what did you do after you finished?"

Ella got up and walked over to the counter to put her now empty cup into the sink. "We talked a little, and then I left. On the way home, I happened to notice my friend Sarah's car parked outside the pub, so I stopped in for a while," she said, not making eye contact with her cousins. She hated lying, but she didn't want to tell them how she had left the cottage last night and driven aimlessly around the back roads, thinking of Gabriel's kiss.

"Is that so?"

"Leave her alone, Jen," Katherine warned her sister.

"I'm just curious," Jen explained innocently.

"No, you're trying to distract yourself from your own problems," Katherine snapped.

"I don't have any problems!"

Katherine rolled her eyes and then made an unattractive pouty face. "'Oh, Nicky, I miss you so much. Please Nicky, help me. Help me. I'm falling...,'" she mimicked her sister while she leaned far over in her chair toward the floor and waved her arms around, as though she'd lost her balance.

"I do not do that!" Jen stated, her face flaming.

"You do. I sleep in the same bed with you, remember?" Katherine insisted.

The girls glared at each other while Ella leaned against the counter, watching them. She wondered if they always fought this way, or if they just saved their shows for her entertainment.

"What's to eat, Mommy?" Calvin stumbled into the kitchen at that moment. He ignored the snarling faces of Jen and Katherine, his only concern being his empty stomach.

Ella welcomed the interruption. "Good morning, sleepyhead." She went over and knelt down, giving him just a quick squeeze, knowing how he shunned public displays of affection.

"What would you like to eat this morning?"

"Any of that cereal left?" he asked, meaning the cereal that his watch had come in.

"No, I'm afraid it's all gone," Ella told him.

"Hey, kiddo. How about I make you some French toast?" Katherine asked, reaching out to ruffle his hair.

Calvin made a face. "No thanks. I still feel kinda sick from that popcorn you made last night."

Jen laughed out loud over that, glad it was her sister's turn now to be embarrassed.

"How about pancakes?" Ella suggested.

"Okay!" Calvin yelled. He stepped over to the table and slid onto one of the chairs.

Ella poured him a glass of juice, then grabbed some eggs and milk from the fridge. While she mixed the batter her cousins made small talk with Calvin. He told them about Mrs. Mackenzie and the boy who lived next door to her. Ella smiled over his boasts about how he had to be the leader every time they went on a walk together through the woods.

"They'd be lost if I didn't show 'em where to go," Calvin told them gravely.

"My goodness, it's a good thing they have you along, then," Jen said, making her blue eyes wide in awe.

Calvin leaned far back in his seat. "Yep. Sure is. Just like how Mister Gab-real needed me to show him around too," he bragged.

"You don't say?" Katherine exclaimed, pretending she hadn't already heard about him offering his services as a guide to Gabriel.

"Yep. Mommy even had to get me new boots for my job."

Then he was gone, rushing from the table only to return moments later wearing his new boots. He strutted around the kitchen like a bow-legged cowboy in a spaghetti western, his face stern as he came to an abrupt stop before the girls. His hands were on his hips and his legs spread wide as he struck a serious pose.

It was hard to keep a straight face.

After breakfast, Katherine asked Calvin to take her on a tour through the forest behind the house, which gave Ella a chance to escape to the grocery store. Jen had gone off earlier to the bedroom to have a good cry. It seemed that Calvin's boots had reminded her of Nicky.

Ella wasn't certain just how long her cousins planned on staying with her, so she made her meal selections carefully. She still had most of the money Katherine had given her since she'd only spent thirty dollars on their lunch in town. She had also put fifty dollars away so that she'd be able to spend a little on Calvin at the jamboree.

She planned her menus as she went down the aisles, choosing dishes that would be filling but not expensive. Spaghetti was one of her favorites, so she grabbed a large bag of pasta knowing that she had plenty of homemade sauce. Whole chickens were on sale, so she picked up two of them, one to roast and the other for stir-fry or for soup, to use along with the vegetables in her garden. Apples weren't very expensive this time of year, and homemade pie or apple crisp would be nice for dessert, she thought as she wandered the fruit and vegetable section. For a treat, she bought a bunch of grapes, knowing they would bring a smile to Calvin's face.

Later, as she sat at the picnic table in the backyard and watched her son stuff the grapes into his mouth, she wondered if Gabriel would still come with them to the jamboree on Saturday. The way she'd left things with him, she wasn't certain if he ever wanted to see her again, never mind go anywhere with her. She cringed when she recalled the argument they'd had after she'd pushed him away during his second kiss and turned her back on him. When he'd asked her what was wrong, she'd weakly explained that she didn't want the complications of a relationship in her life right now. But he'd guessed the real reason for her hesitation.

"When are you going to stop using your husband's death as an excuse to not get close to anyone?" he'd asked her gently, but she could detect the frustration in his voice. When he failed to get a response from her, he went on. "If anything, losing your husband should have shown you how frail life is.

Nothing is certain. None of us know how long we have, and we need to cherish each moment."

"So, in the meantime I should just go along for the ride, and hope to God that I don't get hurt in the end?" She had spun around and fired the words back at him.

"I'm not going to hurt you, Ella," he'd insisted, taking her shoulders into his grip to stop her from turning away from him again.

"You're still going to leave when the summer is over, and here I'll remain." She'd waved her arm around, dramatically gesturing to their surroundings. "And what about Calvin? Since you have everything worked out, have you thought about what I'm supposed to tell him?"

When Gabriel had failed to answer right away, Ella had stormed off, stating, "I'm not a summer fling!" When she'd heard his approaching footsteps, she had run and jumped into her car, the sound of his shout not halting her flight. She had driven away into the setting sun like a coward. And now, all she could do was reassure herself that she had done the right thing.

~*~

"Are you upset about something, Ella?" Katherine asked. It was Saturday, and her cousin sat beside her as she drove them all to the jamboree.

"Why would you think that?" Ella asked, forcing a smile to her tight lips.

"You're awfully quiet, and you seem pensive."

"Well, I'm feeling sad too, if anyone cares," Jen whined from the backseat.

Katherine turned to glare at her sister. "What's the

matter? Are the trees reminding you of Nicky?" she asked sarcastically.

Jen didn't reply, but stuck out her tongue instead.

"Oh, you are so immature. It's no wonder Mom and Dad say he's too old for you."

"Katherine, that was uncalled for," Ella chastised. Katherine turned back around as her sister stifled a sob.

"You ain't gonna cry again, are ya?" groaned Calvin.

"N...no," Jen croaked.

Ella looked over her shoulder and caught a quick glance of her son swinging his booted feet back and forth anxiously. His eyes were fastened on Jen's face, watching with trepidation for her next hysterical display. Lately, Ella reflected, it felt as if she had two children instead of just one.

Calvin turned his gaze to his watch. "Hurry Mommy," he urged.

She wasn't sure if he was more worried about getting to the jamboree or getting away from Jen before she had another melt down.

She parked in a large open field that served as the parking lot for the weekend event. Cars were crammed in like sardines, and it appeared as though the entire population of Caverly, along with all the summer tourists, were there. As they wound their way through the field of parked cars toward the entrance, Ella watched the excitement grow on Calvin's face. She knew he couldn't possibly remember very much of coming here in the past with her and Joe—it had been over two years.

The smell of cotton candy and caramel apples permeated the air. The sounds of laughter and screams from the midway echoed around them as they entered the gate. Calvin appeared to want to run in every direction at once, uncertain of where to begin. He pulled Ella's hand frantically as he caught sight of a large hot air balloon off in the distance. Ella knew they offered rides in it, but she searched her memory as Calvin pulled her along, trying to remember how much money it would set her back.

Jen and Katherine didn't take long to decide to go off on their own, and Ella suggested they all meet at the hot air balloon in an hour, it being the easiest landmark to spot. Along the way to the ride, Calvin became distracted by the rows of games. Men and women behind the stalls called out to people as they passed by, enticing them with a chance for victory.

"I wanna win some prizes, Mommy!" he told her.

They lined up for tickets, and after handing over a third of her money for the day, she let Calvin choose a couple of games to play. He soon grew bored when he failed to win anything, so she let him ride on the ponies and then they braved the Ferris wheel together. While they swung precariously up high looking out over the jamboree, Ella scanned the parking lot for Gabriel's car. She thought she detected a black sports car that looked just like the one he drove, but she couldn't be certain.

She didn't know what she would do if she ran into him here today. Should she greet him kindly and pretend as though nothing had happened between them? Or should she ignore him and cross her fingers that Calvin didn't catch sight of him?

An hour after their arrival she led Calvin toward the hot

air balloon, which was tied in an open field at the far side of the grounds. Calvin watched in amazement as the balloon crept steadily up into the sky. A man and woman with their two young children waved excitedly from above to the people below. Thick heavy ropes, the width of a man's arm, secured the balloon to keep it from flying away, but Ella still had misgivings about letting her son get into it.

Jen and Katherine were waiting for them. Katherine watched the balloon, waving to the people in the basket, while Jen flirted outrageously with the handsome young man in charge of the ride. It amazed her that her cousin could so quickly forget her own insistence that there was no other man on earth who could even remotely compare with her long-lost Nicky. *Oh, to be young again*, Ella thought wistfully.

"I wanna go up there," Calvin declared, awe in his voice. He stood with his feet braced far apart and his head tilted way back, one hand fisted at his hip while the other shielded the sun from his eyes.

Ella swallowed hard. The balloon strained against the bonds that held it, making a creaking noise that grated on her nerves. It was no higher than the Ferris wheel, but it was not the height that bothered her. It was how the little basket waved around ominously, as though it were magically suspended in air. The balloon itself looked sturdy enough, but what if the basket broke away and tumbled to the ground?

Katherine must have noticed the frown of worry she wore. She reached out and gave Ella's hand a slight squeeze.

"You don't have to go up, you know," Katherine told her.

"Tell that to Calvin," Ella replied.

The ride cost five dollars a person, which really wasn't

an exorbitant fee for a once in a life-time experience. There was a bit of a line-up, though, so she didn't have to make up her mind right away. Perhaps something else might catch the interest of her son, or she could tempt him with the offer of an early lunch. Ella made the suggestion, and after Katherine agreed it was a good idea, Calvin reluctantly let them lead him away. It took a bit more persuading, however, to pry Jen from the side of her newest admirer.

They settled on root beers and sausage on a bun. Tables with umbrellas were set up out front of the little trailer that sold them the food, and they sat there while they ate. Calvin was halfway through his lunch when a big black dog meandered over to them, wagging its tail back and forth. Before Ella could stop him, Calvin broke off a piece of his bun and threw it to the animal, who snatched it up in his powerful jaws and swallowed it quickly. As she chastised him about feeding other people's pets, the dog sat down beside their table. Ella was about to shoo the animal away, certain its owner must be looking for it, when she gazed into its big brown eyes.

They stared back at her with more emotion than she thought possible for an animal. She was instantly captivated by that stare, and to Calvin's delight she found herself feeding it pieces of her own bun.

"Can we keep him, Mommy?" he asked her excitedly.

This was her own fault, Ella thought. She had wished for something to come along to distract her son from going up into that balloon ride, and here it was. She petted the dog on his head, deciding he seemed friendly enough. "I'm sorry, honey, but he must have an owner."

"He isn't wearing a collar," Jen pointed out.

"That doesn't mean he doesn't belong to someone." Katherine glared at her sister.

Ella looked around, hoping to catch sight of someone who looked as though they were searching for a lost dog. Calvin's face was set in that "I have to have it" pout, and Ella knew she was going to be in for a fight soon if she didn't get him away from the animal. The balloon ride suddenly didn't seem quite so intimidating now that she was faced with the prospect of lugging home another mouth to feed. And by the appearance of the creature, she was sure he would devour a lot.

To her relief, the dog dashed off in another direction as soon as it noticed they were out of food.

"You see," Ella told Calvin, who watched the dog with longing as it scurried around the other tables. "He probably belongs to the man who sold us the sausages."

"I suppose," Calvin agreed grudgingly. "Hey, can we go up in the balloon now?" His face lost its frown and lit up with excitement as he recalled the ride.

She sighed. It seemed there was just no getting around it. "Oh, all right."

Calvin jumped quickly to his feet and began to lead the way over to the balloon, which they all could see floating high up in the cloudless blue sky.

As they approached the ride, Calvin hurried over to get into line. Jen rushed over to stand beside the muscular young man she had left earlier. Katherine and Ella walked over to stand with Calvin as they waited their turn.

Ella turned to Katherine, and she could see her cousin was even more nervous about going into the basket than she was. "You don't have to go up with us," she told her.

"I know. It's just that Jen has done so many adventurous things, and she's always telling me how boring I am. For once, I'd like to do something exciting."

Ella tilted her head to look up at the balloon, and suddenly wished the line would move faster so she could get this over with.

As the next people began their ascent, Calvin tugged on Ella's sleeve and gestured upward. Ella looked across the open field and saw a small plane coming toward the jamboree. They watched as it came up quickly and then dropped low, as though it would land in the field. It began tipping from side to side, as if it were waving to the crowds of people, before it again climbed up high above the ground. For a moment, Ella wondered if the fair might be offering rides, but as she saw it race across to the other side of the field again, she figured it was most likely putting on a show. The plane engine roared as it swung back around and, to their amazement, it suddenly flipped over when it got close by, so it was upside down, then it zoomed back away from them. Everyone watched, enraptured by the unexpected display, and Ella could hear Jen exclaim to her new friend that she didn't realize there would be an air show this year. It did make her wonder when the young man replied that he didn't know anything about it.

"Mommy, look!" Calvin yelled.

Ella followed his anxious gesture, and to her dismay she saw the black dog they'd fed earlier running out onto the field barking fiercely at the plane. But that wasn't all she saw. When she searched the slowly gathering crowd of onlookers for a sign of the dog's owner, her gaze fell on Gabriel, who was standing not more than twenty feet away. He was looking right at her.

Ella abruptly turned away. She knew she was being rude to not acknowledge his presence with a wave or a smile, but she didn't know what else to do. When she finally gained the courage to look back in his direction, he was gone. Her eyes darted around as she tried to find him, although she knew it was pointless — the damage had been done.

Suddenly, Katherine gasped and cried out, "Oh, no!"

Ella turned to see what had upset her, and as she followed her cousin's line of sight, she spotted the object of her dismay. It was Calvin. He had run off into the field to go after the black dog, who was still frantically barking. Ella looked up to gage the direction of the plane, but it was not a threat to her son for it was now several thousand feet up in the air. The man wearing a parachute, who had launched himself from the plane's side door, *was* a threat, however.

Ella didn't hesitate before she tore onto the field. The dog had turned his attention to the man falling from the sky and raced toward him, while Calvin, unaware of the danger, flew across the field as fast as his booted feet would carry him.

"Calvin!" Ella screeched, trying to make her voice heard over the roar of the crowd. If he heard, he ignored her.

Ella noticed the man in the parachute was trying to change his direction after spotting them, but he appeared to be having some difficulty. His parachute was giving him trouble and he was coming down quickly.

Finally nearing her son, who had mercifully slowed down, she wasted no time in reaching out to shove him forward. Calvin landed hard on his bottom, and turned his head just in time to see the man from the plane crash into his mother.

~*~

The impact sent her careening to the ground. It didn't take long for her cousins and Gabriel, who had joined in the race, to reach her side. When Jen went to lift Ella's head into her lap, Gabriel ordered her to stop.

"Don't move her. She may have broken something."

"Somebody call an ambulance!" Katherine screamed at the crowd, most of who were now rushing toward the fallen pair lying motionless on the ground.

Gabriel took control of the scene, telling Jen and Katherine to keep the people back. Others who had now arrived helped to hold back the rush of onlookers who gathered around them. Jen went to Calvin, who sat frozen in shock, and took him into her arms, holding him tight, telling him over and over that his mother would be all right.

Katherine, thankfully into her second year of nursing college, rushed to tend to the fallen man, who had begun to stir and was pulling at the parachute harness that was fastened around him. She helped untangle him and sat him up gently to unhook the harness, her eyes darting every few seconds toward Ella, who still lay silently on the ground.

Calvin broke free of Jen's arms and ran to his mother's side. Gabriel was bent over her, feeling her limbs to check for broken bones.

"Please, make my mommy better," he pleaded with Gabriel.

~*~

Ella could faintly hear voices, seemingly from far away, urging her to wake-up. As the voices grew louder the pain she had retreated from began to return. She didn't want to wake up if it meant feeling such pain again, but then she heard a voice. It stood out from all the others, and Ella knew she could not return to the darkness. She had to awaken, for the fear she heard in her son's voice she could not bear to ignore.

"Mommy!"

Ella began to stir and her eyes fluttered open. She tried to focus on Calvin's tear-filled gaze from where he stood beside Gabriel.

"Can you hear me, Ella?" Gabriel asked her, his voice filled with concern.

"Oh, Ella! Are you all right?" yelled Jen as she rushed forward.

"Ella, please, say something," called Katherine from the side of the man who had wreaked such havoc.

"I...I'm okay," Ella said.

Just then a man began to push through the crowd, demanding to be allowed forward. "I'm a doctor!" he yelled when two men tried to halt his advance. They let go of him and he hurried over to Ella's side.

"Can you tell me your name, miss?" he asked, kneeling beside her.

"Ella," she replied faintly, while he gently opened her eye wider to gaze at her pupil.

Gabriel stood up and backed away from her then, giving the doctor room to look her over.

He reached out to place his hands on Calvin's shoulders, and gave him a comforting squeeze. Calvin tilted his head back to look up into Gabriel's face. "You saved my mommy," he told him.

Seeing that she was all right, Ella saw Gabriel's worried

95

look swiftly replaced by one of rage.

He turned and glared at the parachutist, who seemed to be none the worse for wear as he carefully gained his feet with the aid of Katherine. He was a large man, just slightly shorter in height than Gabriel. He had a lean athletic build, and was a quick healer, it seemed, for he had already shrugged off Katherine's assistance and walked in a circle, testing his legs.

Gabriel stalked toward the man, and when Jen saw the look of intent on his face, she quickly rushed after him. The parachutist was now bent forward and attempting to pull off his helmet. Gabriel had taken up a stance before him and blocked the man from Jen's view.

Ella feared what Gabriel would do, for she knew he was greatly angered over the man's carelessness. She saw Jen attempt to catch Gabriel about the arm, but he pulled free of her grip and she stumbled forward, just as the man pulled his handsome face free of the helmet.

"Nicky?" Jen gasped, just as Gabriel's fist slammed into his jaw.

Chapter Seven

Ella was resting quietly at home, feeling content to allow her cousins the responsibility of running the household. It was Sunday, and as she lay in her bed she welcomed the calm of the early morning.

After the incident yesterday, Caverly's only ambulance had arrived on the scene shortly after Gabriel had knocked out Nicky. She and Nicky had been loaded up and whisked off to the Hospital, and were admitted for observation. While she was there, Calvin had stayed with her until he had grown tired and hungry, and Katherine, who had driven Ella's car to the hospital, had taken him home for dinner. Jen had stuck her head in the door of Ella's room every half-hour to check on her, but had spent most of her time hovering over Nicky.

After Nicky had been deemed fit for release, he had walked hesitantly into Ella's room, wary of Gabriel's presence. Gabriel had left to grab a bite to eat, and Nicky had taken advantage of his absence to offer his heartfelt apologies.

She'd taken pity on the man after seeing the black eye he sported and the sincere regret on his face. She'd given him her forgiveness, although, if it had been Calvin that he'd plowed into, she would not have been so magnanimous. He had thanked her profusely with his adorable Australian accent, and then quickly fled her room. Ella hadn't been surprised when Jen rushed off after him.

Ella was released later in the evening, and after everyone had gone to bed, Jen had arrived home. She'd popped her head in the door of Ella's room and asked if she was settled in. When Ella had patted the side of her bed as an invitation for Jen to join her, she had timidly entered within. After sitting down, Jen had promptly broken into tears. She'd admitted between sobs that everything that had happened was all her fault, since Nicky had performed the stunt to win her back.

Ella had told her that she couldn't be responsible for the actions of someone else, especially when Jen had no idea what Nicky had been planning. The problem with men like Nicky, Ella had informed her younger cousin, was that they sometimes did thoughtless things and could act with great immaturity. Although, it seemed he had received his just rewards. Katherine had told her last night that the Caverly police hadn't been as charitable toward him as Ella had. They'd slapped Nicky with a five-hundred-dollar fine for performing his little stunt. Ella could only hope that he'd think twice before doing anything so reckless again.

Thinking about last night, she suddenly remembered how strangely Gabriel had behaved yesterday. He had followed the ambulance to the hospital, and remained at her bedside for hours throughout the long afternoon. After returning from his dinner, he stayed until she was released.

He had not spoken a word of how she had ignored him at the jamboree, or how they had quarreled the other night. Instead, he had treated her as though she were a delicate flower to be handled with utmost care. He'd driven her home and, to her humiliation, even carried her inside the house and placed her in her bed. She smiled as she recalled how kind he had been.

A knock on her door interrupted her thoughts, and Ella called out to enter. She wasn't surprised to see Katherine, because Calvin wouldn't have knocked and Jen was most assuredly still in bed. Katherine carried a tray with her breakfast on it, and Ella felt a mixture of guilt and pleasure over the attention she was receiving. She knew she was going to find it very difficult to remain in bed for the next couple of days as the doctor had ordered.

"How are you feeling today?" Katherine asked her, concern etched on her face.

Ella reached out to steady the tray Katherine placed before her on the bed. "Much better this morning, thanks. My head hardly hurts at all now."

"Well, you just eat up, and you'll be back on your feet before you know it."

Katherine was wearing Ella's apron and had a smudge of flour on her cheek. It appeared she'd made pancakes for breakfast. However, as Ella regarded her plate, she thought it might be French toast instead. It was hard to tell from the way everything was fused together by the burnt edges. The coffee seemed to look all right until Ella noticed there was a tea bag floating in it.

"This looks...delicious," she lied while smiling brightly up at Katherine, who was watching her anxiously.

Katherine beamed. "I'll leave you to it then. Calvin will be up any moment now, and don't you worry, I'll see he cleans his plate this morning."

"Make sure you pour him a big glass of milk," Ella called out to her retreating form.

After Katherine was gone, she wasted no time in setting her tray aside and climbing out of bed. She eased her window up quietly and tipped her plate behind the bushes planted below.

Her coffee-tea went out next. By the time Calvin burst through her door howling his complaints, she was neatly tucked back in her bed.

"Mommy, I can't eat something burnt that ain't marshmallows!"

His brown hair was still tousled from his sleep, and Ella could tell by the way his shirt was unevenly buttoned and how the zipper on his shorts hung wide open that he'd attempted to dress himself. She reached out and started to fix his buttons while attempting to reason with him.

"Honey, you're going to have to be on your best behavior for Katherine and Jen while I rest, all right?"

"But I'm starvin', Mommy, and I can't eat that scary stuff Katherine makes. You shoulda seen what she made me for dinner last night—I still don't know what it was."

Ella sighed. "Jen should be up soon. You could have some fruit until then," she told him, knowing Jen would refuse to eat Katherine's cooking as well.

"Calvin?" Katherine called.

They could hear her coming down the hall toward Ella's room, and Calvin didn't waste any time jumping into the closet.

"Don't tell her where I am!" he hissed, before he shut the door tight.

Katherine knocked on her door and Ella told her to come in.

"I can't find Calvin," she said. "He was in the kitchen sitting down at the table one minute, and the next minute he was gone."

"Don't worry, I just saw him. Perhaps he's just too anxious to eat. Why don't you go ahead and get ready for church?"

"Church? I can't go to church and leave you here all alone."

Ella opened her mouth to argue, but the doorbell suddenly rang. Katherine gave Ella a hard look, which told her she wasn't finished with this conversation, then she rushed off to answer the door.

Calvin jumped out of the closet. "If you want me, Mommy, I'll be in my own closet," he told her, and started off down the hallway toward his room.

Jen appeared at her door then. "Wait till you see what Katherine's done to the kitchen," she said, wearing a lofty smile.

Ella sighed and leaned deeper into her pillows. If this was any indication of the peace and quiet she could expect to get, she might as well just get up.

Katherine came in next. "You have a visitor," she announced.

She stepped further into the room to allow the visitor to

101

enter. Ella wasn't too surprised to see Gabriel appear, carrying a huge bouquet of red roses.

He gave Ella a quick smile and then darted a look at Jen. He'd discovered last night it was her precious Nicky that he'd knocked out, and he appeared uncertain of the greeting he may receive.

Jen eyed him and then walked over to stand before him. "These are beautiful!" she announced, gifting him with a dazzling smile.

The whole room seemed to breathe a sigh of relief.

"We haven't been formally introduced," Jen told him, offering her hand, which Gabriel promptly shook. "I'm Ella's cousin, Jen, and this is my sister, Katherine." Her other hand gestured toward Katherine, but her gaze remained on Gabriel.

Ella didn't miss the way Jen's hand continued to hold onto his.

"A pleasure to meet you," he responded. "I'm Gabriel."

Katherine took his hand next, after getting her sister to finally move aside, and thanked him for all his help yesterday. "We'd have been lost without you," she told him. She took the roses from his hand, saying she would put them in water.

Ella realized with all the excitement yesterday, there hadn't been time for proper introductions. Jen excused herself, leaving Ella and Gabriel alone together, but not before giving him one last lingering appraisal. The silence that suddenly flooded the room made Ella uncomfortable. Gabriel pulled up a chair beside her bed and sat down, his eyes never leaving hers. Ella was embarrassed over his scrutiny. She could tell he was noticing the large bruise on the side of her face that had turned an ugly purple overnight. When she'd stumbled into the bathroom in the middle of the night, she'd switched on the light and seen her face. It hadn't been pretty. She could imagine how she must look to him now, with her hair all askew from a restless sleep and her purple face. She was amazed he hadn't run from the room yet.

He took her hand gently in his and brought it to his lips to kiss softly. "How are you this morning?"

"F…fine," she stammered. "Thank you for the flowers, that was very thoughtful of you."

He shrugged off her gratitude. "Are you in pain?"

"No."

"Can I get you anything?"

"Besides being a little hungry, I'm all right."

"You haven't eaten yet?" Concern pinched his brow.

"Well, Katherine made breakfast earlier, but I wasn't really hungry then. I'll make up something after they go to church," Ella told him.

"You can't stay here alone," he informed her.

She was getting tired of being told that. Didn't anyone realize it was the only way she'd ever get any rest? Then an idea occurred to her. She could at least convince Katherine to take Jen and Calvin to church if Gabriel stayed with her. But they would have to go outside, because she didn't want to stay here alone with him in her bedroom.

"How about I put on a robe and you can sit with me outside in the yard, then?" Ella asked him. Gabriel grinned wolfishly, and Ella knew he understood that she preferred to not be alone with him in the house, and especially not while she lay in her bed. She waited patiently while he stepped from the room before she slipped out from beneath the covers.

Her nightgown was thin but long, reaching down past her knees, and when she put on her robe she felt she was decently attired. Her slippers went on next, and Gabriel stood ready outside the doorway, gallantly offering his arm for assistance.

He led her along the hallway and down the few steps toward the living room. As they passed through the kitchen, Ella said a quick hello to Jen, who was sitting at the table munching on some toast.

"What are you doing out of bed, Ella?" Jen asked, trying to make her voice stern.

"The fresh air will do me a world of good," Ella responded, not slowing her gait toward the back door.

When she stepped outside she noticed Katherine right away. "Katherine, you can go to church. Gabriel has offered to stay with me...." Her voice trailed off as she peered across the yard. It was the bark of a dog that had gained her attention. As she looked closely she noticed it wasn't just any dog, but that great black beast from the jamboree. Calvin was trailing the animal gleefully across the yard, feeding it pieces of toast.

"What in the world is that dog doing here?" Ella asked aloud.

"I don't know," Katherine admitted.

Gabriel noticed the look on Ella's face. "Isn't that Calvin's dog?" he asked, obviously confused. "I saw him chasing it across the field and I just assumed it belonged to him."

"No, it's not our dog," Ella said, watching Calvin pet the animal lovingly. "We fed it a little of our lunch yesterday and it followed us over to the balloon ride. When Calvin saw it go after the plane he feared for its safety, and that's what started the whole mess."

"Oh, no. I'm sorry Ella, I really thought he was yours. I spent most of the evening looking for him after I left here, thinking Calvin would be heartbroken if he lost his pet."

"It's not your fault, Gabriel. I don't know who the dog belongs to, but perhaps I could place an ad in Caverly's paper. The owner will surely come forward to claim it."

"Good idea. I could take him back to the cottage with me if you like while you wait for the owner to call."

Ella turned to watch Calvin again, and smiled over the way he had knelt down to wrap his arms around the dog, who was licking his face with his big red tongue. She still had some money left over from the money Katherine had given her, so buying a couple of cans of dog food wouldn't set her back too much, she decided.

"No. I think Calvin would enjoy having a pet around. Even if it's only temporary." Ella had no sooner said that when the dog broke free of Calvin's grip and dove into the bushes beside the house. She could have died on the spot when the animal reappeared with a large piece of her breakfast in his jaws and began devouring it. Katherine had been watching, and gave Ella a glare as she stomped past her on the way into the house.

"What was that about?" Gabriel asked.

Ella shrugged her shoulders, too embarrassed to explain. She gestured to a couple of folding chairs that were leaning against the side of the house. "Let's sit down," she suggested.

It took another five minutes before Calvin noticed his mother and went over to stand by her chair. "Mommy! See the dog? I heard him bark from my room, and when I ran outside Katherine saw me."

"Gabriel made a mistake, Calvin. He thought the dog belonged to you, that's why he brought him here," Ella told him gently, wanting to prepare him for her next words. "The dog doesn't belong to us, though, and his owner must be worried about him."

Calvin was listening but his eyes were now on the dog that had run over to join them. "Well, we could tell the owner that the dog is here," he suggested.

"That's a good idea. I think we should place a found ad in the paper, and if the owner reads it he can call."

"Yes, and we can tell him that his dog wants to live here now."

Ella sighed. Perhaps keeping the animal here wouldn't be such a good idea after all, she thought. Calvin had only spent a few minutes with it, and already he was becoming too attached. "Honey, you know we can't keep the dog. It wouldn't be fair to him. I'm at work all day, and you're at Mrs. MacKenzie's house."

"But we're here now," he whined.

"Yes, that's why I thought we might let the dog stay while we search for his owner. But if you're going to get too attached to him, I'm afraid Gabriel will have to take him over to the cottage."

"I won't get too 'tached. I promise, Mommy," he vowed. He then turned and ran back across the yard, laughing as the dog whizzed quickly past him.

Gabriel had been silent throughout their little exchange, and Ella appreciated that he hadn't tried to step in this time and fix things for her. When she looked at him she saw he was watching her strangely.

"What is it?" she asked.

"Nothing. I'm just so relieved that you're okay. You gave us such a fright yesterday."

Ella felt self-conscious as he continued to stare at her. "I think some good came out of what happened, actually," she told him.

His look became puzzled over her statement. "What good could possibly come from getting your head smashed against the ground by a reckless fool?"

"It made me realize what you said the other day was true."

"What I said?"

"That life is uncertain. You have to grab onto every bit of happiness that comes your way."

He just stared at her, and Ella didn't know what he was thinking. She was about to ask him when Jen came out the back door and walked over to them.

"Katherine wants to go to church now. I think she's angry about something, but I don't know what," Jen informed her.

"Calvin," Ella called. When he ran over to her she asked him to run inside to get ready for church.

"But who'll watch Samson?"

"Who's Samson?" Ella asked, but her question was soon answered when the black dog ran over to them and dropped down at Calvin's feet.

So much for Calvin not getting too attached.

After Katherine, Jen, and Calvin left for church, Ella and Gabriel sat companionably side by side, enjoying the morning. The dog, newly christened Samson by Calvin, had gone off to lie under a tree in the shade.

They were silent for a while, content to enjoy the beautiful morning while the warm sun caressed their faces. The silence didn't feel awkward. It felt comfortable, as though they were a couple that had been together for years.

Ella turned her head to regard Gabriel, and was surprised to see that he was watching her intently. "What is it?" she asked.

"I'm thinking about what you said to me earlier, before Jen came outside."

Ella thought for a moment before she replied. "Oh, about life being uncertain?"

"Yes. And I agree, but I came to another conclusion after what happened to you."

"And what would that be?" Ella asked carefully, not certain she liked the sound of his voice.

"I came very close to understanding what it was like for you—to lose someone, I mean," he explained. When he saw by her confused expression that she didn't know what he was getting at, he went on. "I know it wasn't the same extent of what you experienced, of course. But I still felt as though someone had reached inside my chest and pulled out my heart."

"Do you mean you thought I had died?" Ella asked, incredulously.

"Either died, or had been terribly injured."

"You're comparing what you went through yesterday to what I felt when I learned of Joe's death?" She couldn't believe what he was saying. It wasn't possibly the same! She had loved Joe. They'd been married and had a child together. But she didn't feel angry with Gabriel for comparing the two scenarios. What Gabriel had implied, but had not quite said, was that he cared for her—a lot.

"I think you were right to not want a more involved relationship with me," Gabriel told her.

Ella couldn't believe his words. He had practically just confessed how much he cared for her, and in his next breath he was telling her they should not become closer. The accident had made her see how wrong she had been to shut out the possibility of having love in her life, but at the same time, it had shown Gabriel how painful love can be—especially if you could lose it so easily. She couldn't win. She didn't know what to say to him. How could she make him see that he was wrong to fear love, just as she had been?

She reached out and took his hand. It felt warm and strong in her grip, and she gave his fingers a little squeeze. When she looked up at his face, he was not looking at her—instead, he was staring at their joined hands. When he finally did meet her gaze, his eyes were filled with tenderness and his lips were turned up slightly in a warm smile. Ella felt her heart clench in that moment. How could she lose him now, when she had finally knocked down the barriers she'd placed around her heart? Was she destined to forever lose the ones she cared for?

"Ella?" he said softly, breaking the chaos of her thoughts.

"Yes?"

He didn't say anything else, just sighed deeply, leaned toward her, and surrendered to feelings he couldn't deny. Their kiss seemed to last forever, neither wanting to break the contact.

Gabriel abruptly pulled away and stood up, putting

distance between them. Ella looked up at him as he faced her with a tortured expression.

"I'm sorry. I didn't mean to.... We can't."

"Gabriel, don't turn away from me," she begged him.

He ran his hand through his hair from force of habit, forgetting that he had it tied back. When his hand became tangled, he grew frustrated and pulled at the tie with his other hand. He wound up snaring the tie in the back of his hair and had to use both hands to try and free himself.

Ella took pity on him and rose to grasp his hands. "Let me," she said.

He stilled finally, and leaned his head down so she could work on the hopeless knot he'd made. After a few moments he was free, but Ella came around in front of him and placed her hands on the sides of his face, trapping him once again.

Gabriel closed his eyes when she gazed at him heatedly, and she could hear his half-hearted attempt for her to stop, but she kissed him anyway, deeply and as passionately as she could.

She told him with her kiss what she could not say to him with words. Soon he was kissing her back, answering her silent plea.

They separated a few minutes later, breathing heavily, but remaining close enough for Ella to lean her head on his chest. She could hear his heart pounding, the fast rhythm matching hers.

"I guess I'm doing a bad job at just being your friend," he sighed.

"I'm glad."

He wrapped his arm around her waist and eased her back

down into her chair. "You're supposed to be resting."

"I'm tired of resting. I'm ready to eat, I think."

"Let me run into town and grab us something from the restaurant," he suggested. "Unless, of course, you want me to salvage what's left of Katherine's cooking," he teased, staring over toward the bushes.

Ella laughed and blushed at the same time, remembering her embarrassment. "I'd better make dinner tonight, or else Children's Services may come knocking on my door for child abuse."

It was Gabriel's turn to laugh. "Why don't I come back tonight with dinner? We could eat outside. Make a picnic of it."

She smiled up at him. "Calvin would enjoy that."

She felt lighthearted all of a sudden. It was as though a river of emotions dammed for too long had finally burst forth and flooded her with happiness. Her heart swelled, drinking deeply, for it had too long been denied. Gabriel had done this for her, she realized. He had broken down her resolve, and made her feel things she'd sworn never to feel again.

After they ate an early lunch, he left for the cottage and Ella went to lie down in her room.

She knew it wouldn't be long before Katherine and Jen came home with Calvin, and she wanted to enjoy the peace and quiet while she could.

Gabriel had gone to Mom's Restaurant in town and ordered enough chicken sandwiches to feed a small army. He'd also brought back a big wrapped package of wedge fries, and cold tubs of macaroni salad and coleslaw. There was enough food left over to feed everyone lunch when they returned, and Ella could only hope that Katherine wouldn't be too offended. Calvin, on the other hand, would be delighted to be spared the torture of eating another meal made by Katherine.

Ella heard them arrive and put on her robe to join them. "Where's Jen?" she asked, looking around the kitchen.

Katherine rolled her eyes. "Guess who was standing on the steps to the church when we came out?"

"Nicky?" Ella ventured a guess, although she knew what the answer would be.

"Yes. He waited out there because he didn't know if he'd be welcome. At least that's what he told Jen before they ran off together. I could tell by the way he was looking around that he was really just afraid that Gabriel might be with us."

Katherine spotted the food in the fridge, and to Ella's relief, she didn't make any comments, just started putting it out on the table. Calvin, who had taken a seat, his arms crossed and his face set in a defiant frown, suddenly became animated with joy when he saw the restaurant food being laid out before him.

"All right!" he yelled. "Are you gonna eat, Mommy? It's lunch time," he stated, looking at his watch.

Ella took a seat beside him and poured him a drink after Katherine put the milk on the table.

"No. Gabriel and I already had some," she said, warily watching Katherine for a reaction to her words.

"That was nice of him to pick up lunch for everyone," Katherine admitted grudgingly.

"He thought you could use a break," Ella said gently, not wanting to hurt Katherine's tender feelings more than she already had.

Katherine took a seat and smiled tightly. "It's okay, Ella. I get it. I know I'm a rotten cook."

"You're not," Ella insisted.

"Yeah, she is," Calvin remarked.

Ella shot him a quelling look that made him duck his head and shove more fries into his mouth. "You're good at so many other things, Katherine."

"Yes, I suppose so. I can't expect to be good at everything, right?"

"Right," Ella quickly agreed. "So where did Jen and Nicky go?" she asked, changing the subject.

"Who knows? They're probably off on some big adventure, knowing Nicky."

Ella wasn't as quick to shrug off Jen's whereabouts as Katherine obviously was. Caverly wasn't exactly a big town, but there were plenty of things to do here that would certainly tempt a daredevil like Nicky.

Julie Parker

Chapter Eight

Gabriel returned to Ella's house at five o'clock with dinner, much to the relief of Calvin.

He'd been watching for his car through the living room window for over an hour, peering over his shoulder every few minutes at the kitchen to make sure Katherine wasn't cooking them something.

Ella was up and dressed, to the dismay of her younger cousin, who kept insisting that she should remain in bed. "I'm fine," she told her again as she went to open the door for Gabriel.

They spread a blanket on the grass in the backyard, and Ella helped him lay out the food he'd purchased in town.

"This looks delicious," she told him, eyeing the sliced roast beef, baked potatoes, fresh carrots, and corn. Warm rolls rounded out the meal, and he'd even brought a blueberry pie for dessert.

Katherine had joined them and she agreed with Ella.

114

Calvin didn't need to voice his opinion.

It was obvious by the way he eagerly eyed the food that he was thrilled with the bounty before him. Samson was sitting beside the blanket close to Calvin and watching everyone anxiously, hoping for bits of food to drop to the ground as they began to eat.

Halfway through the meal, Jen appeared from around the side of the house. She saw them on the grass and looked momentarily startled. "Oh, hi," she said hesitantly.

Ella soon knew the reason for Jen's nervous behavior when Nicky appeared from behind her.

He took one look at Gabriel and stopped dead in his tracks. The men just stared at each other, their gazes locked in a silent battle. Gabriel was the larger of the two, and when he took to his feet, Ella could tell his size intimidated Nicky. Nicky must have remembered how it felt to be knocked out by him, for he took an involuntary step back. His hand went unconsciously to his face, almost to shield his blackened eye from further harm.

Jen latched onto his arm, not allowing him to retreat. "I think it's time you two officially met," she said loudly.

Ella quickly stood up. She noted the angry look on Gabriel's face, and wasn't sure how he would react to Jen's idea. She placed herself before him and pleaded silently that he not lose his temper. She shot a glance at Calvin and motioned to him to go inside. Calvin sighed and got to his feet, and started for the door after reaching down to grab another buttered roll. Katherine rose and caught up to him, shooting Nicky a glare.

Ella moved to stand beside Gabriel. "Well, then...," she said, attempting to break the tension between the men. She soon became silent, though, when she saw Nicky pull away from Jen's grip and cautiously come forward.

It was soon apparent that Nicky looked upon this meeting as another one of his adventures.

He squared his shoulders and stood up straighter to make his six-foot height seem taller. His blond hair reached his shoulders and curled around his face, giving him a boyish appearance despite his older years. Looking at him, Ella found it hard to believe that he was actually two years older than she was.

Nicky's approach was slow and careful, his gaze never leaving his opponent's face. It seemed like it took forever for him to finally come before them. His hand reached out and Ella saw the slight quiver in his fingers, which belied the fearless stance he'd assumed.

"G' day mate. I'm Nick," he said, offering his hand to Gabriel, who eyed it with annoyance.

Ella held her breath while Gabriel continued to stand still, showing no signs of wanting to take Nicky's hand. When he did finally reach out to take it, she wished he hadn't, for now the two men held on to each other tightly. Too tightly. Ella could see the slight wince of pain on Nicky's face as Gabriel continued to squeeze his hand. She almost stepped in to try and break them apart, when Gabriel finally released him and Nicky quickly stepped back.

"Quite a grip you've got there. You should come climbing with me sometime," Nicky said, rubbing his sore hand with the other. His voice held a touch of amusement while he spoke in an attempt to lighten the mood, but he was ultimately failing. "I'm sorry 'bout the lousy jump I made," he said seriously.

When Gabriel remained silent, Ella hurried to say, "You've already apologized. It was an accident." She directed her words more to Gabriel than Nicky.

Jen walked up to stand beside Nicky and latched onto his arm once again. "Well, now that that's all behind us, I'm sure you two will become the best of friends."

Gabriel shot her a look that said, "Don't count on it" and abruptly turned away. "I need to get going, Ella," he said stiffly, and started walking across the yard.

She hurried after him, sparing Nicky and Jen an apologetic glance. She caught up to him on the driveway. He could hear her approach and stopped to turn and face her.

"I'm sorry. I just worried if I didn't leave, I might do something I wouldn't regret. When I think about what he did to you...."

Ella reached up to touch his face. "No, it's all right. Jen can't expect you to just shake hands and make up as though nothing happened."

"I tried."

"I know you did," she said soothingly. "Just give it some time."

"Yeah," he agreed. He bent his head to brush his lips gently against hers in a kiss goodbye.

"I'll call you in the morning. If you're up to it, I'll take you and Calvin out for a drive if you like."

"I'd like that."

She watched while he opened the door of his sports car and climbed inside, then waved as he drove away. Taking a deep breath, she started back around the house to face her cousin and the man who'd almost killed her yesterday.

~*~

"Around the corner is the road to High Falls," Calvin yelled out to Gabriel from the back seat. He had insisted that Gabriel put the top down on his car for their ride this morning, and the wind was whipping his hair around wildly.

Despite the wind, Ella was enjoying the ride as much as Calvin. She'd never ridden in a convertible before, and it felt as though they were flying down the winding roads outside of town.

Gabriel had picked them up just after nine o'clock in the morning, and asked where they'd like to go. It had been Calvin who chose this road, which was one of his favorites. He called it Snake Road, for it twisted and turned and wound around for several miles. One of the roads that branched off it led to High Falls, as Calvin had pointed out.

"Do you want to go?" asked Gabriel, slowing down and leaning toward her to ask his question so Calvin couldn't overhear.

Ella knew he didn't want to upset Calvin if she wasn't up to it. "If you like. But the road is pretty treacherous," she warned him.

Gabriel smiled and gave her a wink, letting her know he'd take it easy as he turned down the roadway to the falls. It took almost ten minutes of Calvin barking out instructions to reach the small parking area. Ella was pleased to see they had the place to themselves. Being an early Monday morning, she knew not many vacationers would be up and about at this hour. It was the perfect time for sightseeing.

Before Calvin rushed out onto the long concrete dam, Ella grabbed his hand tightly. There was a chest-high fence down the length of the walkway, but Ella still got nervous every time she came here. Gabriel followed them out to the center of the dam and peered at the water draining through the slits.

"Look over here," Calvin told him. "That side's boring."

Gabriel joined them on the opposite rail, and had to admit this was the more interesting side.

"That's quite a drop," he observed aloud.

"Yes, it is," Ella agreed. She leaned against the railing and looked down. The spray misted up to blow gently on her face as she watched the water crashing onto the rocks below. She came here with Calvin at least three or four times a year, but never grew bored with the view. Being here reminded her of the trip she and Joe had taken to Niagara Falls years ago. This manmade waterfall was by no means as grand as the natural falls they'd seen, but she still had a fondness for it. If she closed her eyes, the sounds were almost the same.

"I know what you're thinking," Gabriel whispered in her ear.

Ella smiled at his words, remembering she had told him of her only trip across the border. "If you like this waterfall, then you'd really like the one in Niagara Falls," she told him.

"I guess we'll just have to go there to find out."

She studied his expression to see if he was teasing her, but his face held no hint of laughter.

She wondered if he truly meant he would take her there, and if he did, how would she feel about it? It had been where she and Joe had spent their honeymoon. Could she bear the thought of going there with another man?

"Are you guys goin' somewhere?" Calvin asked. "I'm not gonna get stuck at home with Katherine and Jen, am I?"

119

Ella reached down and tousled his hair playfully. "I thought you enjoyed being with them."

He looked guilty for a moment before he spoke, almost as though he was about to confide a big secret. "Katherine can't cook, and Jen cries all the time."

"Oh," Ella said, not knowing how to respond. She couldn't deny her cousins had their flaws, but they had been a godsend to her the past couple of days. Actually, since their arrival, they'd kept her quite preoccupied with their daily drama, and she'd hardly had time to worry about her own problems.

After spending another half-hour at High Falls, Ella suggested they go and see the huge cave at Trout Lake. "I think you'd get a kick out of it," she said. "I first saw it several years ago, and was amazed by the sheer size of it. It used to be a small cave until they mined it during the war for minerals. Other caves around Caverly were also mined, but this is the largest I've seen. The entrance reaches over thirty feet high, and it's at least one-hundred feet deep."

Gabriel voiced his misgivings about hiking to the cave when they reached a narrow roadway at Trout Lake, and Ella told him they'd have to walk the rest of the way in. She was still recovering from her ordeal, he reminded her, and she was supposed to be taking it easy. Only after she and Calvin both assured him that it wasn't far did he relent.

"You might want to bring your camera," Ella suggested, knowing he'd probably not seen something quite like this before. He pulled a flashlight out of his trunk as well.

Gabriel must have explored many caves in the past, considering the amount of traveling he'd done, but Ella felt this sight was one that would still impress him. The trail led around a corner and as they rounded it, Gabriel suddenly stopped dead in his tracks.

"Wow!" he exclaimed as he stared in awe at the sight before him.

Ella smiled at his reaction, for hers had been similar. "It's something, isn't it?"

"I wasn't expecting it to be so huge," he admitted.

"Are ya comin'?" yelled Calvin, who had run up to the entrance of the cave.

"Calvin, wait for us before you go inside," Ella called out.

"I know, I know."

Gabriel turned to her, his brow creased in puzzlement. "Is something wrong?"

"You can never be too careful," she told him. "There may be a bear in there."

Calvin waited for them to join him at the entrance. He was impatient to go inside, and he tapped his booted foot and stared pointedly at his watch until they reached his side.

"Can I go in now?" he asked.

Gabriel was shining his flashlight around the interior of the cave, and when he gave the all clear, Calvin gave a whoop of joy and ran inside. The first thing he did was race to the back and begin climbing the biggest ledge. When Ella reached the back of the cave he waved to her from above.

"Look at me!"

"You be careful up there. And when you want to get down, tell me so I can help you," she reminded him.

"I will," he said with a sigh.

Ella turned her attention to Gabriel, who was shining his flashlight up against the high ceiling, which reflected his light brightly. He then went to touch the side wall and ran his fingers down the rough edge with wonder. The look on his face was one of astonishment, and Ella was pleased that he found this place as fascinating as she did.

"I've never seen anything like this," he said, turning to face her.

"I know. Every time I come here, it never fails to amaze me."

"Is this quartz?"

"Yes, and some other minerals as well, but mostly quartz. That's what gives the walls and ceiling the glassy appearance."

He walked over to where she stood and shone his light up to where Calvin was perched.

"Come on up," Calvin invited him.

Gabriel didn't need any further urging. He handed his flashlight over to Ella and climbed up to stand beside Calvin.

"Watch your head," she told him, seeing him duck just in time to avoid a collision with a rock sticking out above.

"Pass me the light again, Ella," he said, reaching his hand down toward her. She gave him the flashlight and he shone it against the side of the cave.

"See how it's dug out here?" Calvin motioned to the wall. "They were mining it."

"Incredible," Gabriel said.

It was almost an hour later before they decided to leave the cave. Ella had to promise she'd return so Gabriel could take more pictures.

"I can't believe my batteries died," he told her for the third time.

When they got back out onto the main road to town,

Calvin was full of suggestions of where they could go next. "Wait till we show you the old mines," he said excitedly. "And then we can go up to Eagle's Landing, or take a boat ride on the river."

"Hold on there, kiddo. Your mom needs to go home and rest now. We'll go out another day and do those things, okay?" Gabriel told him.

Ella saw the frown on Calvin's face and felt badly for him. She didn't like having to take it easy, especially when she felt fine and it was her last week of vacation. There wasn't much time remaining, and it felt as though the days were flying by. Before she knew it, she'd be back at work. Jen and Katherine would probably be leaving soon, and Calvin would be spending his days at Mrs. MacKenzie's house. She didn't want to waste her time resting, she wanted to be out enjoying herself with Calvin and Gabriel. Ella almost suggested as much, but when she saw the stubborn look on Gabriel's face, she knew he would only insist that he return them home.

She leaned back in her seat and decided to enjoy the ride, reminding herself it was still only Monday, and they had the rest of the week to go exploring.

That evening, Jen approached Ella while she was starting to fix dinner. She was hesitant and seemed a bit uneasy, and Ella knew there was something on her mind.

"What is it, Jen?" she asked kindly.

"It's about Nicky. I was wondering—if it's not too much trouble, that is—if he could maybe stay for dinner tonight?"

"I think that would be fine," Ella told her. She had planned on serving fish tonight, and though it wouldn't be gourmet, there was certainly plenty of it, so she didn't see a problem with having Nicky join them.

Jen breathed a sigh of relief. "Great. Can I help you with something?"

"Sure, how about you grab a bowl and pick some fresh string beans from the garden?"

Calvin entered the kitchen and Jen asked him if he'd like to join her.

"Nah, I wanna play with Samson," he replied as he went out the back door.

"That reminds me," Ella said to Jen. "I called the paper this morning and placed an ad before I went out. If anyone calls about the dog, please let me know, okay?"

Jen was watching Calvin race around the yard with Samson through the back door. "Sure, although you're going to be in for a barrel of tears if someone claims that dog."

Ella pulled the fish out of the fridge and put it on the counter. "I know," she sighed.

"Maybe you could get Calvin a puppy of his own," Jen suggested.

"No. I can't—" She caught herself before she said that she couldn't afford it. "It wouldn't be fair to the dog," she said instead. "I'll be back at work next week, and Calvin will be at Mrs. MacKenzie's house after you and Katherine go home, so there'll be no one here to take care of it."

"Yeah, I guess you're right. It's too bad, though—Calvin really likes having a pet."

"Maybe I'll get him a fish," Ella said, eyeing dinner on the counter top.

Nicky was full of stories that night as they sat around the table. Jen hung on his every word, as did Calvin, who had been quickly won over, but Katherine spent most of the evening rolling her eyes. Ella found Nicky to be charming, and the stories he told reminded her of Gabriel's adventures. Though Gabriel would find it ironic, it appeared he and Nicky were very much alike.

They retired to the living room to sit by the fireplace for coffee after dinner. Ella allowed Samson inside, and Calvin was soon rushing off to show the dog his room. Katherine also decided to head off to the bedroom she and Jen shared, making an excuse that she felt a headache coming on.

"Dinner was delicious, Ella. Thanks again for inviting me," Nicky said politely.

Ella was glad dinner had run so smoothly. She'd been worried an argument would break out between Katherine and Nicky, or that Calvin would say or do something to upset the meal. Calvin had eyed Nicky angrily when he'd arrived, getting a good enough look at him to recognize the man who had landed on his mother. But all had gone well. After Calvin heard a few of Nicky's tales, he'd quickly warmed up to him. There had been no fights or temper-tantrums, and there'd been enough food to go around.

"I'm glad you could join us tonight, Nicky. It was nice getting to know you better."

"I'm sorry your boyfriend is still so angry with me. Although, I must admit, if the roles were reversed, and someone had run into my Jenny like that...." His words had the desired effect, as Ella could see Jen's cheeks turn a light shade of red.

"He just needs a little time," Ella told him. "And he's not my boyfriend."

"Not yet, perhaps," Jen teased her.

"I must say, I've never seen anyone jump from a plane to impress a girl before. What made you think of doing something like that?" Ella asked, ignoring Jen's words.

Nicky laughed a little to cover-up his embarrassment of having his plan to impress Jen turn out so terribly. "I really don't know what came over me. When I drove up here looking for Jen, I passed the Caverly airport and suddenly got this great idea — or so I thought at the time — to jump out of a plane over the jamboree."

"But how did you even know that I'd be there to see you do it?" asked Jen.

"I didn't," he admitted. "I hoped you'd be there, but even if you weren't, I figured my escapade might appear in the paper and you'd see what I'd done."

"Yes, you're right. It's a small town, and people were talking about it. They probably still are," Ella told him.

"You did the most exciting thing this town has seen in years," Jen gushed, latching onto Nicky's arm.

"No, I did the dumbest thing this town has seen in years," Nicky corrected her, looking at Ella remorsefully.

"It was just an unfortunate accident," Ella said. She didn't want to think about what had happened to her anymore. It only reminded her of how it had made Gabriel so afraid of losing her that he'd told her they shouldn't become any closer.

She pushed those thoughts from her mind. After spending this morning together, it seemed the last thing on Gabriel's mind was staying away from her. In fact, after he'd dropped her and Calvin off, he'd asked if he could pick them up again tomorrow morning. Calvin had looked at his watch and told him to come at nine o'clock sharp. Ella couldn't help but smile as she remembered how Gabriel had climbed into his car and given her a wink as he drove away. She believed if Calvin hadn't been standing there, Gabriel might have kissed her goodbye.

"Jen and I were thinking we might head out to the pub. Do you want to come along?" Nicky asked her.

"Yes Ella, would you?" Jen asked.

Ella turned her attention to Jen, who was giving her a strange look. It took a moment for her to realize Jen was only being polite with her invitation, and really wanted to be alone with Nicky.

"Oh, no, thank you. Katherine's probably lying down, and I don't want to bother her to watch Calvin. Besides, I'm feeling tired after having such a busy day. I think I'll just go to bed early as well."

"Are you sure?" Nicky asked her.

"Yes, really. You two go on."

Calvin interrupted them. He entered the room followed by Samson, who trailed him faithfully. "Are you going?" His question was directed at Nicky.

"Aye, little mate," he said, bending down to Calvin's height.

"Are you comin' back again?"

"Sure. I'll come back again soon. Maybe you can show me around the forest out back?"

"Yeah. I could do that," Calvin told him. He shook Nicky's hand and then gave Jen a very quick kiss goodnight. "Katherine's wrong about you. You're not a dumb jerk, I think you're neat," he yelled before running off to his room

127

with the dog.

~*~

When Gabriel arrived the next morning, the first place Calvin wanted him to see was Eagle's Landing. Gabriel was silent as they drove through town and up the steep roadway to the top of the high hill overlooking Caverly. Ella could tell by the thoughtful look on his face that what ever had captured his attention the day before was still on his mind today. When he'd dropped them off yesterday, he'd been quite anxious to return to the cottage for some reason, despite having enjoyed their outing.

It was a warm and beautiful sunny day, with hardly a cloud in the sky, and Ella knew the view would be great. Calvin talked the entire trip, his words spoken loudly so he could be heard over the rush of the wind. They parked the car when they reached the top of Eagle's Landing, and began walking up the winding trails to look at the view. Ella waited until Calvin was just far enough ahead of them for her and Gabriel to have a conversation in private.

"Are you all right?" she asked him. Gabriel turned to look at her, and she was surprised to see that her question had startled him. It was as if he had been on autopilot for the last fifteen minutes and had finally noticed she was at his side.

"Sure," he replied.

"Okay. What's the matter?" Ella stopped walking so that she was certain he was giving her his full attention. Her eyes quickly searched for Calvin, and she spotted him not too far ahead, crouched down before a wild raspberry bush.

Gabriel stopped also, becoming fully focused on Ella. "Why do you think something is wrong?"

"It's you. You're acting as though you're not even here."

"I'm here. I admit, I have a lot on my mind, but I enjoy being out with you and Calvin."

Ella laughed over his defensive tone. "I'm not accusing you of anything, Gabriel. I just couldn't help but notice how distracted you are. I thought, perhaps, you might have changed your mind and wanted to do something else this morning besides going sightseeing."

Gabriel absently handled the camera that hung around his neck. "I...," he began, his voice faltering while his face suddenly became lit up with excitement. "I didn't want to tell you this yet. In case it didn't work out. But yesterday, while we were in the cave, something came over me. It was like how I used to feel when I was getting a great idea for a story."

"You mean, you felt inspired?"

"Yes. I was inspired. I went home after I dropped you and Calvin off, and I sat out on the deck with a pencil and a notebook and began jotting down ideas. I was there for hours. It was as though all of a sudden I'd become flooded with ideas, and couldn't get them down fast enough."

"That's great."

"What's great?" Calvin asked. He had approached them, and now looked around the spot where they stood. "I don't see anything so great."

"We're talking about grown-up things, Calvin," Ella explained.

"Oh, you mean boring things," he said, then ran back off toward the raspberry bushes again.

Ella turned to Gabriel and smiled brightly at him. She was relieved he was over his writer's block. "I'm happy for you," she told him. "It's great that the cave inspired you to write again."

Gabriel reached out and took her hand while looking tenderly into her eyes. "No, Ella. It wasn't the cave that inspired me. It was you."

Chapter Nine

"Now you're the one who looks miles away," Gabriel teased Ella as they sat beneath the umbrella table at the ice cream shop in town. He'd leaned over to whisper in her ear, and when she jumped slightly from the sound of his husky voice, he gave her a little wink. Calvin sat, oblivious to them both, busy licking around the edge of his cone to catch the drippings.

Ella was still mulling over the words Gabriel had spoken to her at Eagle's Landing. He had caught her off guard with his admission, and she'd not known how to respond. Instead of saying anything to him, she had quickly turned her attention to Calvin, who had wandered farther off down the trail. She had shot Gabriel an apologetic glance and hurried off after her son. When Gabriel had caught up to them, they were near the edge of the cliff, and he'd been easily distracted by the fantastic view before him.

But now all of his attention was on her, and what he'd

told her an hour ago. She wasn't worried he would elaborate on his words, not with Calvin so close-by, but Ella knew she shouldn't become so distracted that she didn't enjoy their time out together. Silently her heart soared. She'd longed to hear such words from him. She hoped it meant he realized he'd been wrong to say they should not be together—that he'd had a change of heart. She smiled at him, and Gabriel reached beneath the table to take her hand, out of Calvin's line of sight.

"So, what now?" he asked. Ella was unsure of how to respond to his question, and when he noticed her look of confusion, he made himself clearer. "Where would you like to go next?"

"Oh," she said, feeling slightly embarrassed. She had thought for a moment he'd been talking about their relationship.

Calvin had no hesitation about where he'd like to go. "I wanna show you the waterfall at Loon Lake."

"Oh, Calvin, no, not today. That's an all-day trip. We should save that for another time," Ella told him.

Calvin's pout of disappointment turned to a happy grin when Gabriel offered an alternative.

"How about we take a boat ride on the river, and we could go to the waterfall at Loon Lake tomorrow?"

"Are you certain you want to tie up an entire day like that?" Ella asked him, knowing he must be anxious to get back to the new book he had started on.

"I have all evening to write," he assured her.

Ella was silently relieved Gabriel hadn't said he wanted to spend the rest of the summer working solely on his novel. It would have given him the perfect excuse to keep his distance from her, if that's what he'd wanted.

After Calvin finished his cone, they drove to a spot beside the river that rented out boats. They were soon settled into the seats of a long blue canoe and paddling their way down the river that wound around Caverly. It was a better way to see the town, Ella reflected, without having stop lights to contend with, not to mention the congestion of busy roadways from all of the tourists.

As they traveled along, Ella and Calvin both pointed out areas of interest to Gabriel as they glided past them. "There is a bunch of bed and breakfast homes set up in and out of town," Ella told him. "That big old house there used to be one years ago."

"Yeah, the one beside the graveyard!" Calvin yelled. "There's ghosts in there."

"Where did you hear such a thing?" demanded Ella.

"Jen told me."

She sighed as she looked back at Calvin's wide eyes and serious expression. It was going to take a while before she could convince him there was no such thing as ghosts. Although, as Gabriel guided the boat past the funeral parlor and the graveyard, she couldn't help but shiver a little.

"What is that over there?" Gabriel asked suddenly.

"Do you mean the bait and tackle shop? That would be a good place to go next if you want to spend some time fishing on Loon Lake."

"No. I mean over there." He pointed up the river and farther into town, where black smoke was billowing overtop one of the buildings.

Ella looked off into the distance, and for a moment she felt a tingle of dread in the pit of her stomach.

"Mommy! Isn't that —?"

He didn't have a chance to finish his question before Ella interrupted him. "Oh, God!" she said, beginning to paddle frantically to turn them around. Gabriel saw what she was doing, and he began to back paddle on the opposite side to help out.

"What is it, Ella?"

"I think it's the library. Cate and Sarah could still be in there!"

They turned the canoe around and began to stroke swiftly back toward the boat rental shop. Ella knew it would be faster to drive over instead of docking the boat here along the shoreline and hiking across town.

When they finally docked, she hurried to climb ashore and helped Calvin get out of the boat. She didn't waste any time talking with the older man, who had come outside when he spotted their return. She just grabbed Calvin by the hand and rushed to Gabriel's car as fast as she could. Gabriel was right behind her, quickly paying the man for the boat rental.

As they sped toward the burning building, Calvin was uncharacteristically silent, no doubt sensing his mother's fear. Ella bit her bottom lip as Gabriel did his best to maneuver his car around the traffic in town, which was becoming even worse with the arrival of police cars and the single Caverly fire truck.

Gabriel pulled into a used car lot, and they abandoned the car and ran by foot toward the library. As they got closer, Ella noticed a throng of onlookers anxious to catch sight of what was happening. She was grateful for Gabriel's great size and height, for he had no problem easing his way through the crowd and pulling her and Calvin along behind him. They soon were close enough to see the extent of the damage, being careful to stay a safe distance back from the building, which was still billowing large puffs of black smoke from the windows.

The destruction to the books and the building was the least of Ella's worries as she scanned the crowd anxiously for her friends. It was several tense minutes before she saw them huddled together outside, up the street from the library.

Ella pulled on Gabriel's sleeve, doubting he'd hear her over the loud wailing of the sirens and raised voices of the crowd. When he looked down at her, she directed his gaze beyond the policemen, who were trying to keep control of the scene, to her friends. He again was able to clear a path to lead her and Calvin over to Cate and Sarah who, thankfully, appeared unharmed.

Ella rushed forward and hugged them both, sending up a silent prayer of thanks for finding them safe. "Thank God you're both all right! What happened?" she asked them.

Cate was the first to answer. "I don't know. I was in the back room when all of a sudden black smoke began to pour down from the ceiling." She began to cough, and Sarah patted her on the back until she caught her breath.

A policeman approached them and Ella recognized him as he came closer. "Ted, I'm so glad you're here," she said, stepping forward to grasp his hand. Ted had been there to break the news to her two years ago when Joe had died. Brian, another policeman, had also been there, and Ella figured he was probably somewhere amongst the chaos going on. The two officers had been childhood friends of Joe, and Ella had known that being the ones to tell her about his fatal accident must have been the hardest thing they'd ever done.

"Were you in the building, Ella, when the fire broke out?" Ted asked her, concern etched on his face.

"No. I'm on vacation this week. Cate and Sarah were inside."

Ted turned his attention to the other women, sparing only a quick glance at Gabriel and a smile for Calvin. "Can you tell me what happened?"

As Cate and Sarah stepped forward to tell what they knew about the fire, Ella turned her attention to the building, which resembled a smoldering dark shell. Now that she knew her friends were safe, the reality of the situation sunk in. It was disturbing what this fire would mean to her. It could take months to rebuild the library, and in the meantime, she would have no job and no way to support Calvin and herself.

"I think I have everything I need," Ted said, capping his pen and putting his notebook into his pocket. "If you're both certain you don't want to go to the hospital, then I can arrange for a ride home if you like."

"No. Thanks, Ted," Cate said. "We're fine. My car is parked down the side street, and I can drive Sarah home."

"Okay. If you need anything, call down to the station, or else you can call me or Brian at home," Ted told them. He turned to leave, and as he passed Gabriel he gave him a brief nod.

Ella said a quick goodbye and watched Ted disappear into the crowd, knowing now wasn't the time for introductions.

"Ella, what happened to your face?" Sarah asked suddenly.

"A parachute guy landed on her head!" Calvin said.

"He what?" Cate gasped.

"We were at the jamboree, and there was this plane doing what we thought at the time was an air show—" Ella began explaining when Calvin cut her off.

"Yeah, but then our dog ran after the plane and I went to get him. Mommy ran after me and that's when the parachute guy, who is really Nicky, landed on Mommy's head."

"I remember reading something about the parachute incident in the paper, but I didn't know the person hurt was you, Ella. There were no names mentioned," Sarah said.

"Hi. I'm Cate and this is Sarah," Cate said to Gabriel, sticking her hand out for him to shake.

Gabriel smiled charmingly and took Cate's hand, then he reached out to shake Sarah's hand.

"Nice to meet you. I'm Gabriel Stolks," he said.

Both Cate and Sarah gasped at the same time, and said in unison, "*The* Gabriel Stolks?"

Ella laughed at their expressions. "Yes. *The* Gabriel Stolks. He's renting my uncle's cottage," she told them.

"Don't you wanna hear about my mommy's head?" Calvin demanded.

Cate and Sarah promptly turned their attention back to Calvin. "When did you get a dog?"

Cate asked. "And who is Nicky?"

"Now, where was I?" Calvin teased, putting a finger beneath his chin after noticing he had their full attention. "Oh, yeah. The dog is Samson, he's lost so he's staying at our house, and Nicky is Jen's boyfriend. No, maybe he's not her boyfriend. Is he Mommy?"

"I don't know, sweetheart," Ella replied.

"Well, Nicky landed on Mommy's head, and we couldn't go on the balloon ride 'cause we had to go to the hospital instead."

"That about sums it up," Ella said dryly.

Cate began to cough again, and this time Ella was the one to pat her on the back. "Are you sure you don't want to get checked out at the hospital?" she asked her.

Cate waved her hand around dismissively. "No. I think...I'll just go...home," she said between gasps for air.

"I think it's best if we do go home now," Sarah said. "Call me later, okay, Ella?"

"Sure."

Ella could tell by the way Sarah was looking at the library that thoughts similar to the ones she'd had earlier were running though her mind. The building was almost completely destroyed. What the fire hadn't damaged, the water did. The entire building would have to be rebuilt and new books purchased, along with shelves and desks. Everything was gone. It would be a long time before any of them could go back to work.

"It was nice meeting you," Cate said to Gabriel, finally regaining her breath.

"And you. Both of you," Gabriel said, including Sarah.

As they walked down the street to Cate's car, Ella could hear Sarah saying, "Can you believe that was Gabriel Stolks?" She smiled over the way her friends dismissed their obvious distress about the fire after meeting a famous, handsome author. As Ella turned her sights back toward the burned library and felt the familiar feeling of doom in the pit of her belly, she desperately wished she could do the same.

~*~

Early Friday morning Ella lay tucked in her bed beneath the covers, not yet ready to face another day. It had been a fantastic week. She had spent every day with Gabriel and Calvin, exploring all of the wonders Caverly had to offer. They'd seen Loon Lake's waterfall, the Markley Mines, and returned to the cave twice. The past two evenings Katherine had watched Calvin, happily eating take-out food while Ella and Gabriel dined in town. Things had gone so well. Gabriel had been sweet and charming as he regaled her with tales of his exciting new book. This time he had included a love story in his murder-mystery. He'd even hinted that Ella greatly resembled the heroine. Ella feared she was falling hard for Gabriel, and though she kept reminding herself that she had to give love a chance, it was still difficult for her knowing he would be leaving town once the summer ended. But it wasn't the reason she didn't want to get out of bed this morning.

She had come home from enjoying dinner with Gabriel last night, and Katherine had been waiting up for her. She'd received a call from Ella's boss, Mr. Turner. When Ella had called him back, he'd broken the news that she wouldn't be needed back at work for at least three months.

Ella had tried to hide her fear and frustration from Katherine, but she knew by the look on her cousin's face that she understood Ella's situation all too well. Ella had tried to sound upbeat when she told Katherine that she'd enjoy an extended vacation, but Katherine didn't appear convinced.

Ella had gone to bed and lain awake for hours.

So far, she'd managed to keep her financial problems hidden from her cousins and Gabriel. It had been easy with Gabriel—he never let her pay for anything when they went out. He'd even been so kind as to bring the take-out food that Calvin enjoyed so much whenever he picked her up to go out for dinner. But he would notice the For Sale sign when it went up on her front lawn.

She didn't want to do it, but if she kept delaying, the decision would no longer be hers to make.

She finally rose from her bed and got dressed. It wouldn't help matters any lying around feeling sorry for herself. She'd only draw unwanted attention her way.

She went into the kitchen and began opening up cupboards, deciding on what to make for breakfast. She'd been able to pick up a paycheck yesterday from Mr. Turner, who'd paid her until the end of July. Tonight she planned on cooking Gabriel a special meal. First, she'd have to go back to the grocery store for a couple of items she needed. Gabriel had said he planned to spend the evening writing. She wanted to bring dinner over to the cottage and surprise him.

They could enjoy a quiet meal together, and then she'd leave early so he could get back to work.

It was her way of repaying him for all that he'd done for her and Calvin. Perhaps, while she was in town, she'd stop over at the townhouses by the river and see how much the rent was. A town house would be better to live in than an apartment, she figured, since they at least had a little yard Calvin could play in.

"Good morning, Ella," Jen said in a singsong voice.

Ella turned to eye her cousin. She couldn't get over the change in her since Nicky had come to town. Before, she'd had terrible mood swings, one moment laughing, the next crying her eyes out. Now she seemed to float everywhere she went, as though she'd exchanged her legs for a pair of wings. Her crying had stopped, but she still appeared to be on an emotional roller coaster. *It must be love*, Ella thought. She couldn't remember her cousin ever acting this way before.

Jen filled the coffeepot with water and leaned against the counter as she waited for it to brew.

She had a far-off look on her face that Ella couldn't help but notice.

"So, what's on the agenda today?" Ella asked her.

Like her and Gabriel, Jen and Nicky had also been spending a good deal of time out roaming the sights. They'd had a few close calls, arriving at places just as the other couple was leaving.

Gabriel still remained unforgiving of Nicky and his little stunt—it was obvious in the way he'd glare at him whenever they happened to pass each other. Nicky always said hello to Ella and Calvin and would give a polite nod to Gabriel, but he'd been wise enough to keep his distance.

"Yes, do tell us, sister *dear*. What do you and Mr. Wonderful have planned for today?"

Katherine had entered the kitchen and her tone was spiteful and disapproving.

"What do you care?" Jen snapped back.

Ella sighed. She didn't need the aggravation of another spat between these two. As happy as Nicky's arrival had made Jen, it had the opposite effect on her sister. Katherine had been sullen and angry whenever Jen had been around the past week. If Nicky happened to run into Katherine, she wouldn't even try to hide her animosity toward him anymore.

As much as Ella enjoyed having her cousins around, she had to admit she was looking forward to them going home. If she had to sell her house soon, she'd rather not have to explain to them why she was moving. In a few months, after she'd settled into a new place, she would let her aunt and uncle know she'd moved, saying the house had just become too much for her to handle. After all, it was a big effort running a house with all the work to be done, plus raising a child and working full time as well. No one needed to know the truth.

Katherine was ready to give a biting reply to Jen's words when Samson bounded into the kitchen and scratched at the back door to be let out. Ella opened the door for him, then turned to give her cousins a look to silence any further arguing. Calvin would soon enter the kitchen, and she didn't want him to hear Jen and Katherine fighting again. She knew he wouldn't be far behind the dog. They'd become very close, and she was concerned they might be stuck with the animal because no one had answered her ad. That reminded her; when she went into town she would stop by the print shop and ask them to run the ad for another three days. She could check out the help wanted section too. If she got another job, perhaps she wouldn't have to sell her house.

"Morning, Mommy," Calvin said, rubbing the sleep from his eyes as he wandered into the kitchen. He sat down at the table and let out a big yawn before saying hi to Katherine and Jen.

Ella eyed him speculatively after she reached into the

cupboard to grab a bowl for his cereal.

"Didn't you sleep well, sugar?" she asked as she placed the bowl down before him on the table.

Calvin stared straight ahead, his eyes half closed. "Nah. Samson kept jumpin' on my bed and takin' all the covers," he told her.

"I think he'll have to start sleeping in the kitchen," she said, making Calvin quickly alert. He sat straight up in his chair and bulged his eyes open wide.

"No, Mommy. He likes sleepin' with me. He'd be scared out here all alone."

"But if he's not letting you get any rest, he can't stay in your room."

"Your mom's right, kiddo," Jen told him.

"Yes. That's something we actually agree on, Jen. Your mom is right, Calvin," Katherine said.

"What is this? A lynchin'?" Calvin demanded.

Jen and Katherine ducked their heads to hide their laughter at the indignant look on his face.

Ella, however, didn't find her son amusing.

"All right, Calvin, he can have one more chance," she conceded. "But if you get up tomorrow looking like you do now, then Samson will have to sleep in here."

"Okay. Okay."

After breakfast, Katherine drove into town to do some shopping of her own, and Jen went outside to play with Calvin and Samson. She had offered to watch Calvin while Ella ran into town. Jen told her she was expecting Nicky, and that they thought it would be fun to go exploring in the woods behind the house with Calvin. Ella remembered Calvin mentioning something about it when Nicky had been over for dinner. She thought it was a good idea, and it would give her some time to look at the townhouses along the river.

Ella carried a shopping basket in one hand and lifted a tin of sauce with the other to inspect the ingredients. Gabriel had told her he wasn't fond of onions, and she wanted to make sure she didn't include them by accident in her dinner tonight. She was planning on making chicken breast baked in a tomato sauce, smothered in fresh mushrooms. She'd made it before, and with baked potatoes and Caesar salad she thought it would go over well tonight. Garlic bread with cheese would be good too, she thought, and made a mental note to head over to the bakery section next.

This was her last stop before she went home to begin cooking her special dinner. The first place she'd gone was to the print shop to talk to Maria about running her ad again. She'd left with a paper, and while she sat in her car she'd scanned the pages optimistically for a help wanted notice. There had been a few jobs, but unfortunately nothing that suited her. After that she'd gone with a heavy heart to view the townhouses.

She'd stopped by the superintendent's office at the complex to get someone to show her what was available. As she looked around she'd tried to convince herself that it wouldn't be so bad. She'd silently rhymed off all of the positive things, such as all the children Calvin would have to play with. There was a tidy playground packed with children of all ages. Calvin wouldn't be so isolated here, in town. She had ignored the loud bustle of the place, and concentrated on how beautiful the river was. The unit itself, Ella had to admit, was quite roomy.

Something else had happened today that had sent her thoughts reeling. After she left the townhouses she'd headed for the grocery store—feeling desolate and praying for some sort of miracle—when she'd stopped at a traffic light, looked to her left, and noticed a vacant store.

There weren't many stores on the main street considering it wasn't very long. The empty one had once been a bakery. Now it had a For Rent sign in the window.

In that moment, a thought had struck her. She could open her own store—a bookstore—which had always been her dream. She loved books, and her and Joe had collected hundreds of them that now sat in boxes in her basement. The newest big thing in the larger cities was bookstore coffee shops. How cozy they appeared, with their overstuffed easy chairs and little coffee tables set about, surrounded by rows of bookshelves. Caverly was a small town, but many people from larger cities came here in the summer months. And now the winter months were gaining popularity as well with the allure of ice fishing, and snowmobile and ski trails. Opening up something like that, she could host events like book club meetings, author readings, and signing events.

Ella thought about the store while she shopped, and allowed the dream to enlighten her mind with wishful thoughts. Tonight, after bringing dinner over to Gabriel, she'd go home and hash out her ideas. It wasn't so farfetched for her to open a business, especially one that the town would surely make use of considering they'd be without a library for the next three months. If she were to approach the bank with a solid, laid out plan on what she intended for the building, surely she stood a good chance of qualifying for a business loan. A business loan was different than a personal loan, and Mr. Bentley would undoubtedly see the potential for her idea. Ella reined in the excitement that bubbled up inside of her every time the store entered into her mind. She didn't want to get herself all worked up with the idea, especially considering how badly things had gone the last time she'd gone to the bank for money. Instead, she turned her concentration to the dinner she was going to make tonight.

In the bread isle of the grocery store there was an assortment of fresh loaves and buns to choose from. She decided on a couple of sub buns to make the garlic bread with. Now she would need to get some fresh garlic. She headed back over to the produce section, and as she grabbed a plastic bag from one of the aisles she noticed a young boy, slightly older than Calvin.

Ella could hear him arguing quietly with the tall, beautiful blonde woman beside him, who she assumed to be his mother. Ella had never seen the pair before, and guessed they were probably renters from out of town. The look on the boy's face was becoming frustrated, and Ella could tell it was an effort for him to keep his voice low as he continued to argue.

"I'm telling you, Mother, Father doesn't like Brussels sprouts."

Yes, Ella decided when she heard the boy's speech, they were not from around here.

His mother was doing a good job of ignoring her son's disapproval. Ella couldn't help but watch and admire her as she continued to keep calm and controlled while her son's voice became increasingly louder. The woman moved farther

SEND ME AN ANGEL

down the aisle and began inspecting broccoli heads, which seemed to meet with her son's approval. "Father does enjoy those," he told her.

Ella was glad the boy had calmed down; she knew all too well how difficult it was to shop with an unruly child. She turned her attention back to the garlic cloves, and decided to buy only one bunch as she didn't use it often.

"No! No onions! You know how much Father hates them," the boy yelled suddenly.

Ella's head snapped up when she heard what he said. She couldn't explain why, but she suddenly had a terrible feeling in her stomach. Gabriel hated onions, but he wasn't the only person who did.

The woman had taken a bag of onions despite her son's vehement objections, and quickly made her way over to the check-out aisle. Ella was also ready to check out, so she stood in the same line as the woman and her son, who was now sulking. It wasn't crowded in the store, but there were still two other people ahead of the woman, and when she began to talk quietly to her son, Ella couldn't help but overhear their conversation.

"I want you to remember to be on your best behavior this week, Darius."

"I know, Mother," the boy responded with a sigh.

"Remember not to upset your father with needless questions. And don't mention a thing about his writing," she instructed him.

Ella felt as though someone had punched her in the stomach. The woman had said not to mention writing! Gabriel was a writer, and he hated onions. This was more than a coincidence, she suddenly feared.

"Do we have much farther to go, Mother? I'm tired," the boy whined.

"No, darling. We'll be there shortly," she told him, smiling beautifully.

And then they were gone. The woman checked out and left the store, while Ella stood stiffly in line, clutching her shopping basket to her breast, staring after her.

"Ma'am?" the girl behind the counter said, drawing her attention.

Ella put her basket down and began to quickly take out the items she had so carefully chosen.

The girl seemed to take forever to ring her through, and when she finally got out to her car, she noticed a sleek black car pulling out of the lot.

Ella quickly tossed the bag of groceries into the back seat, not caring that the garlic rolled out onto the floor. She climbed behind the wheel, and before she had time to rethink her actions, she headed out and began following the black car.

Chapter Ten

Ella pulled her car over to the far right-hand-side of the dirt road leading into Loon Lake. She had driven past the turn-off to her uncle's cottage, and followed the road further on to park her car out of sight. She left her car and traveled by foot back toward the turn-off, keeping close to the edge of the forest in case she needed to quickly hide from sight. After following the other car onto this road, there wasn't any more excuses she could make to herself about the woman's destination. But still, until she was absolutely certain, she would not abandon hope.

She had to know.

She stepped into the woods and wandered as close as she dared to observe her uncle's cottage. Her foolish heart remained optimistic that somehow, someway, she had been mistaken.

But it was not to be so.

As she peeked around the thick tree before her, she sucked

in her breath sharply, for there was the black car sitting in her uncle's driveway. The woman must have arrived just moments ahead of her, considering she had followed her closely.

Ella watched as the woman walked to the back of the car and opened the trunk. She felt her stomach clench when she saw her pull out a large suitcase and place it on the ground. The back door of the cottage swung open and Gabriel stepped outside, calling out a greeting. The boy, Darius, ran from his mother's side and yelled, "Father!" before he barreled into Gabriel's arms. Darius had put down the bag he held in his hand from the grocery store before he ran to Gabriel. He now walked back and reclaimed it. "Mother is going to make us dinner tonight," he said. Now that Ella saw them together, she noticed the obvious resemblance of father and son.

"You're going to cook?" Gabriel asked the woman, flashing her one of his handsome grins.

The woman laughed and put her hands on her hips in mock outrage. "I've spent a little time in the kitchen, I'll have you know."

"Yes, I remember having to put out a lot of fires."

"Well, you're in for a treat tonight."

"Mother bought onions," Darius told him, making a sour face.

Gabriel made a face too, causing Darius to break into peals of laughter.

Ella couldn't believe what she was seeing. It was as though a movie scene was playing out before her eyes. Why had Gabriel not told her he had a wife and child? There had been nothing in his words or actions even hinting at the possibility he had a family. He wore no wedding ring, he had no photos of them lying about in his car or in the cottage that she had ever seen.

There had been nothing, no signs at all.

Gabriel hugged the woman briefly then picked up the suitcase. Ella watched as he led the pair inside. When she finally broke from her trance, she began to back away. Her legs felt weak as she staggered through the woods. She stepped out onto the dirt road and headed slowly toward her car. What a fool she had been, she berated herself. How could she have thought that a man like Gabriel would be interested in her? A plain, small town girl who had nothing to offer him, not compared to that beautiful, glamorous blonde who could have only of been his wife. His wife! How could Gabriel have kissed her the way he had when he was married?

She drove home in a daze and pulled into her driveway. She climbed out of the car and took several steps toward the front door before remembering the groceries in the back seat of her car—the groceries for the special dinner she'd been planning on making tonight for Gabriel. She grabbed the food, having to reach far beneath the seat to find the garlic. Once inside, she piled the items on the counter in the kitchen. Calvin and Jen weren't back from their hike yet, she noted, gazing out the window into the backyard.

Ella was relieved she wouldn't have to deal with anyone right now. She needed to be alone to think about what she had just seen. She walked to her room and once inside, closed the door behind her. What she wanted to do was throw herself down on the bed and cry her eyes out. She sat down and almost gave in to her grief when she heard a quiet knock on her bedroom door. Swallowing back the sob that threatened to erupt from her throat, she called out, "Yes?"

"Ella?" Katherine's voice sounded through the door.

Ella sighed and got up to open the door. "I thought you were out?" She faked a smile while she questioned her cousin.

Katherine wandered into the room when Ella stepped aside. "I was, but instead of shopping I went for a drive, to think."

"What were you thinking about?" Ella asked her, wishing she would leave her alone.

"I'm going home," Katherine announced.

"You're leaving?" She knew Katherine and Jen would eventually return home, but she'd not thought it would be so soon.

"I can't stand to watch my sister make a fool out of herself with that jerk."

"Nicky?" As if she had to ask.

"Yes. He's been here less than a week, and already they're right back to being a couple again. I thought Jen had learned her lesson the first time, but I see I was mistaken."

"Have you asked Jen if she's ready to leave then?"

"No. I'm going home without her," Katherine told her bluntly.

Ella sat back down on her bed again. "Do you really think that's wise? I know you're angry, but sometimes when people get mad they do things in haste they might later regret." She had to keep her mind off all the terrible things she was planning on saying to Gabriel, and perhaps listen to her own advice.

Katherine was pacing the room in agitation. "I know what

I'm doing. Besides, it's not like I'm leaving her stranded — she has Crocodile Nicky to drive her home."

Ella noted the bitterness in her cousin's voice. "I'm sorry you want to leave. I was enjoying having you here, and so was Calvin."

Katherine looked at her with sudden regret. "Oh, Ella, I'm sorry. We really have been terrible company for you, haven't we?"

She stood to place a comforting arm around Katherine's shoulders and gave her a slight squeeze. "Not at all. It's been so nice having you both here," she reassured her.

"Well, then, I'm already packed. I just need to say goodbye to Calvin, and as soon as Jen returns I'll tell her what I've decided." Katherine smiled sadly at her and then walked from the room, leaving Ella alone once more.

She sat down and tried to think about Gabriel, but Katherine's sad face kept entering her thoughts. She couldn't possibly have a good cry now. Too much was going on at the moment.

She couldn't even begin to think about plans for the bookstore. Calvin was sure to return with Jen soon, and Nicky would most likely be with them. And when Katherine told Jen she was leaving — well, Ella knew it would definitely hit the fan then.

She might as well go ahead and prepare the special meal she'd been planning. It might only be her and Calvin that would enjoy it tonight, but she wouldn't let Gabriel's deception drive her into despair. No, she thought, standing up and starting off toward the kitchen, she would go on with her life and forget all about Gabriel Stolks.

Twenty minutes later Calvin crashed in through the back door. "Mommy!" he yelled. He looked around until he spotted Ella, and then ran over to stand before her. "Guess what, Mommy?"

"What?" She could hear Samson scratching on the door and she walked over to let the dog inside. He wagged his tail frantically while he drank sloppily from his water dish, getting more water on the floor than in his mouth.

"Nicky says I'm the best tracker he's ever seen," Calvin bragged.

"He does, does he?" Ella said, sounding impressed.

"Yeah. He said he was a tracker in 'stralia, but he says I'm even better 'n him."

"Calvin, where's Jen?" Ella asked. She'd just put the chicken into the oven, and they had about an hour or so before they ate. She was hoping Katherine would tell Jen how she felt before then. Ella was counting on the girls to work things out so they could all enjoy a nice, peaceful dinner together.

"Jen and Nicky left, Mommy," Calvin told her, walking over to open the fridge.

Ella got him a cup from the cupboard and poured him some apple juice. "Where did they go, did they say?"

Katherine chose that moment to walk into the kitchen. "Where is she?" she asked Ella.

"Hi, Katherine," Calvin said.

"Hey, kiddo." She knelt down before him. "I'm going home now, buddy."

"But you can't go home. Jen's gone out with Nicky. He's real cool."

Katherine visibly cringed. She gave Calvin a quick hug,

and then stood back up to look pointedly at Ella. "See what I mean?" She left the room, and Ella knew she was going to get her suitcase.

Ella walked out to the driveway to say goodbye and Calvin followed along. He was confused that Katherine was going to go home and leave Jen behind.

"Jen is gonna be mad," he said.

"No she's not, Calvin," Ella quickly assured him. "Jen wants to stay here longer with us, but Katherine is ready to go home. Nicky can drive Jen home."

"Oh," Calvin said, smiling because it meant he could spend more time with Nicky.

Their goodbyes were brief. Ella could tell Katherine was anxious to leave, perhaps to avoid a scene with Jen if she happened to return. She drove away after promising to call as soon as she arrived home. Ella knew it would be difficult for her to have to explain to her parents that the impetuous Nicky was back in their daughter's life. Her aunt and uncle hadn't relayed how they felt about Nicky, but if it was anything like Katherine's feelings toward him, Ella knew Jen was in for an earful when she returned home.

An hour later, she and Calvin enjoyed a quiet dinner together. Afterward, they sat in the living room and watched TV for a while. Around eight o'clock, she gave him a bath before reading him a couple of stories and putting him into bed. Katherine called to let her know she had arrived home, and after speaking to her, Ella watched the news and then retired around ten.

She laid quietly in the dark thinking about what had happened to her today.

Her night had ended much differently then she had thought it would. If it hadn't been for the untimely arrival of Gabriel's family, she might right now be sitting under the stars wrapped in his arms. She sighed deeply and rolled to her side. It was probably better not to think about what might have been. What she had witnessed today had changed everything. The sad part about all of this was that she had finally allowed herself to let someone into her life. It had been her misfortune that she'd taken a chance on the wrong man.

"Ella?" a voice called to her from the darkness.

She sat up abruptly in her bed. "Yes?" she answered.

The bedroom door opened a crack and Ella could see Jen peek her head inside the room to peer toward her bed. "Are you awake?"

"Come in, Jen," she said, knowing she must have gone to her room first and noticed Katherine was gone. She reached over to switch on the lamp by her bedside, and shifted over to allow Jen room on the bed. Jen sat down, and when Ella saw her face she could tell she'd been crying. She felt badly for her, knowing how hard it must be to realize she'd been ditched by her own sister. She reached out to give Jen's hand a comforting pat.

"Don't be upset. It's probably for the best things turned out like this," she told her gently. "Look at it this way," she continued. "Now you have more time to spend with Nicky. You're welcome to stay here as long as you like." She would worry about how she'd explain the For Sale sign that ultimately must go up on her lawn when the time came.

Jen looked startled for a moment before she replied. "Ella, it's not Katherine's leaving that has me upset," she said. She stood up and began pacing back and forth before the bed.

"Jen, if that's not what's troubling you, then what is it?" She asked.

Jen stopped and stared at the floor for a minute. Ella was about to ask her the question again, thinking she might not have heard her, when Jen suddenly lifted her head to look Ella directly in the eye.

"I'm glad Katherine's gone so she doesn't have to find out that I'm pregnant."

~*~

Ella sat at the kitchen table the next morning, holding a cup of coffee and staring at a piece of toast. She'd been up since five-thirty in the morning, and decided she should put something else into her stomach besides the two cups of coffee she'd already had. She still couldn't believe what Jen had revealed to her last night.

After telling Ella about her condition, Jen had admitted she wasn't entirely certain she was pregnant, but only suspected. She had then fled the room, leaving Ella to ponder this new dilemma alone. As if she didn't have enough to worry about.

The first thing she needed to do was go into town and pick up a pregnancy test at the drug store. It wouldn't open until eight o'clock, so she still had another half hour to wait. Jen, of course, was still asleep, having blissfully passed off the job of worrying about the problem to Ella. She would have to wake her soon, though, so she could keep an eye on Calvin when he awoke.

As if her thoughts had conjured him, her son entered the kitchen rubbing his eyes. Samson barreled past him and rushed straight for the back door, and Ella rose to let him out.

Calvin slipped into the chair across from hers, and when she turned to walk back to the table, he sat up and bulged his tired eyes wide.

"Dog not letting you get any sleep again?" she asked suspiciously.

Calvin, no doubt remembering her threat yesterday, gulped and opened his eyes even wider.

"I slept fine," he lied. He stifled a yawn by biting down on his lip.

"I can see that. What would you like to eat this morning?" She would save the battle over the dog's sleeping arrangements for tomorrow. The last thing she wanted right now was to have an argument with Calvin.

"How 'bout toast, please?"

Ella passed her toast to him and then went to the fridge to get some jam. She didn't have an appetite anymore, not after suddenly remembering the little boy she'd seen yesterday. A little boy who was probably enjoying his own breakfast right now, with Gabriel.

She pushed the thought of Gabriel from her mind and, after smothering Calvin's toast with jam, strode purposefully to the room Jen slept in. Giving a quick knock on door, she entered, not bothering to wait for an invitation.

Jen lay upon the bed on her side with her knees pulled up tightly against her chest in the fetal position. Her short black curls fanned around her face, making her appear younger. Ella felt a wave of pity wash over her before she reached out and yanked the covers off her.

Jen awoke with a start and sat up abruptly. "What...?"

"Time to get up. I need you to watch Calvin while I run

into town."

Jen rubbed her eyes the same way Calvin had, and Ella was reminded by that small gesture just how young she was. She still had her whole life ahead of her. Finishing college, a career teaching as she had planned, dating, falling in love, becoming engaged, and one day getting married and starting a family. Everything could change if she was pregnant.

Ella drove to town at eight o'clock and picked up the pregnancy test. When the girl behind the counter raised an eyebrow over the purchase, Ella felt obliged to explain that it wasn't for her. The last thing she needed in this small town was a rumor being spread that she was pregnant. She drove home with a heavy heart, and when she pulled up in front of her house she was shocked and surprised to see Gabriel's sleek black car parked in the driveway. She wanted to keep driving as a wave of panic overtook her, but she fought the urge. What was he doing here? For one crazy second, while she eased her car up alongside his, the idea that he'd brought his wife and son over to introduce them entered her mind.

She warily climbed out of her car, the bag with the pregnancy test grasped tightly in her grip, while she scanned the area for signs of the unexpected visitor. Perhaps he was out back, she thought while she ducked in the front door quickly. She snuck toward the kitchen and peeked out the window to see if she could spot him.

And there he was.

She could see him clearly, sitting at the picnic table with Jen across from him. He looked at ease, and even laughed at something Jen was saying. He did not have the look of a man who was about to wreak havoc with her heart. She could also see Darius, and to her surprise, he and Calvin played companionably with Samson. But where was his wife? Ella peered in every direction of the yard before she finally reached the conclusion she wasn't out there.

Finally gaining the courage to leave the house, she put Jen's test on top of the fridge and eased the back door open to step outside. Gabriel didn't hear her approach as she crossed the short distance from the house to the picnic table. Jen spotted her and smiled a greeting, which Gabriel noticed. He turned to look at her over his shoulder.

Ella could tell by the way his expression changed when he saw her that he had much to say.

Though her legs were itching to take flight to carry her away from his words, she walked up bravely to stand before him.

"Hello," she said pleasantly, keeping her shaking hands behind her back.

"Hi," he replied smoothly.

Their eyes locked for an uncomfortable moment until Jen, sensing the tension between them, interrupted by clearing her throat.

"I think I'll just head out front and see if Nicky is here yet," she said.

At the mention of Nicky's name, Gabriel's gaze broke from Ella's and his head snapped around the yard in agitation, as if hoping to spot the offender. "He's coming here?" he asked, the disdain obvious in his voice.

Ella feared it would be a losing battle to try and get the two men to like one another. She watched as Jen quickly rose from the picnic table and, without answering Gabriel's question, walked stiffly toward the front yard.

Ella felt badly for her. She knew it must be difficult to know that almost everyone thought her boyfriend was a jerk, especially now since she believed she was carrying his child. Ella liked Nicky, despite what everyone else's feelings were, having formed her own opinion of him. He was a bit of a showoff and definitely reckless, but she sensed he had a heart of gold, and Calvin adored him.

She looked at Gabriel and felt her heart contract. He was everything she wanted, but he was no longer hers to love. He had a family. "Aren't you going to introduce me to your son, Gabriel?" she asked him.

Though the tone of her voice hadn't been accusing, his face, as he stared back into her eyes, appeared culpable. "I should have told you sooner," he began.

Not wanting to make the moment any easier for him, she remained silent.

He stood up, his eyes darting between his son and Ella. "I hadn't planned on things turning out this way."

"What way? You mean with me finding out?"

He gestured toward the boys, who still played with Samson. "I wanted to tell you about Darius," he insisted. "It's just the timing was never right."

"The time had to be right to tell me you had a son?" Ella asked incredulously. She couldn't imagine any parent not wanting to sing the praises of their child.

"In the beginning the mood between us was almost tense. I knew you were keeping me at a distance, and I understood. But then things changed and we began to get closer. I felt badly I hadn't told you about my son right from the start, and

161

then I worried telling you would have made you turn away from me again. I was afraid I'd waited too long, and I didn't know how to breach the subject."

"So you decided to not tell me at all?" Ella demanded, careful to keep her voice low so the boys wouldn't overhear her anger.

"No. I decided to have him come up here for a visit so that I could introduce you."

"Are you going to introduce me to your wife too?"

Gabriel appeared taken aback by her words. "My wife?"

"I saw them, Gabriel! I saw them at the grocery store and I heard them talking. I knew they were up here to see you." She left out the part about her following the pair to the cottage, not wanting to appear paranoid.

Understanding dawned on his face. "Ah. That's how you knew about Darius. The woman with him is his mother, but she's not my wife."

Could it be true? she wondered. "Well, she seemed to know an awful lot about you."

"That's because she's my ex-wife," he explained. "Her name is Sonia. We had dated only two months when she told me she was pregnant. We decided to get married, thinking it was the best way to handle things, but we were wrong. The marriage only lasted a year."

Ella sat down on the bench seat of the picnic table. Gabriel sat down beside her. He took her hand and looked at her. "Sonia left this morning. I asked her a few days ago to bring Darius up here for a week to spend some time with me."

Ella softened toward him, realizing it must be difficult to be separated from his son. "How often do you see him?"

Gabriel exhaled loudly. "Not as much as I'd like to," he admitted. "Sonia is a model, and she spends a lot of time out of the country. Coordinating our schedules has been difficult over the years. We both have apartments in Toronto, so I took a chance she'd be there and I called. I got lucky," he said, looking over his shoulder toward his son.

"Yes, you did," Ella told him, following his gaze.

"He looks like me, I think," he said, pride evident in his voice.

She smiled over his undisguised vanity. "He does."

He leaned forward and rested his forehead against hers. She closed her eyes and breathed deeply as relief washed over her. Though his reasoning was misguided when it came to his explanation about Darius, she could forgive him for it. It was strange, though, knowing he had a whole other life she knew nothing about.

As though he'd read her mind, he moved back on the seat and said to her, "I worried about what you would think when I told you I had an ex-wife. I failed in that relationship, and I was afraid you would assume I would ultimately fail you too. I worried I might scare you off before you even had a chance to get to know me. That's why I didn't tell you in the beginning."

"I wouldn't blame you for your marriage not working out, Gabriel."

He ran his hand through his hair, which he'd left unbound this morning. "I know that now, but I wasn't sure of it before. I'm sorry I handled things so badly, I just didn't know what else to do."

She admitted to herself that she had made things hard

163

for them to be together in the beginning, and she could understand his hesitance in revealing his situation. Now she wanted to put the unpleasantness aside and concentrate on meeting Gabriel's son. She was slightly nervous about the way the boy would react to her. "Have you told him anything about me?"

Smiling over her anxious expression, Gabriel was quick to reassure her. "Yes, and he'll adore you, as I do." He reached out to hold her gently in his embrace, and Ella placed her hands on his broad chest and leaned into his warmth. He bent down toward her, and as she lifted her face he pressed his lips against hers. The moment was broken by Jen's loud voice.

"Everyone's in the backyard, Nicky," she yelled, as if to give fair warning of their approach.

Ella pulled away when she felt Gabriel stiffen after hearing Nicky's name.

As they rounded the corner Jen continued to walk toward the pair, but Nicky came to an abrupt halt. His eyes were locked on Gabriel, who was returning his stare. Their looks were hard and measured as each sized up the other, as though they were contenders in a wrestling match. Nicky began to stalk forward until he caught up with Jen. Moments later they stood before the picnic table.

"Hi, Nicky," Ella said kindly, hoping to ease the tension.

Nicky's smile flashed quickly at her as he returned the greeting. "G' day, Ella."

Gabriel rose slowly to his feet and Ella sprang up to stand beside him, tucking her hand beneath his arm in an effort to keep him calm. She squeezed his elbow when he failed to acknowledge Nicky's presence. Gabriel looked down and gave her a wink before he returned his gaze to the man before him. He cleared his throat as if he were about to say something that was giving him difficulty. Before he could get the words out, Nicky put forth his hand.

Ella and Jen watched the two as the tension seemed to mount almost unbearably. Then slowly, very slowly, Gabriel reached out his hand and finally took Nicky's. This time he didn't squeeze too hard, and the look of relief on Nicky's face was paramount. The girls both released breaths they'd been holding as they watched the men's faces break into friendly grins.

"How about I run inside and make us all some coffee?" Ella asked.

"Sounds great," Gabriel told her as Nicky nodded his head in agreement.

Ella asked Jen if she'd like to help her, thinking that now would be a good time to let the men have a moment alone to talk things out. They started to walk inside when Ella stopped.

Perhaps she should call the boys inside for a snack, and she could spend a little time getting to know Gabriel's son. She turned to scan the yard, certain the boys were still running around with Samson, as she'd last seen them. When she didn't spot them, her gaze strayed to the back of the yard and the high fence that separated them from the forest. The gate was swung wide open.

"The boys!" she cried suddenly.

Gabriel became alarmed at the look of fear on her face. "What is it?" he asked, catching her arm as she began to run past him.

She yanked free and continued sprinting toward the back

of the yard. "The boys are in the forest!"

Chapter Eleven

Gabriel didn't waste a moment running up alongside Ella as she raced toward the open gate. Before they could dash into the forest beyond, they were joined by Nicky. They stopped after running only a few meters into the woods, calling loudly to the children. "Calvin! Darius!"

Ella's face was contorted with fear as she found herself living a mother's worst nightmare.

Gabriel saw the look and quickly offered her reassurance. "Ella...Ella!" He called loudly to get her to focus on him. "They couldn't have gone far." His eyes were scanning the forest as he spoke.

Hearing the logic of his words, she nodded. He was right of course, she knew, for how far could two little boys have possibly gone in just a few minutes?

"Jen will stay at the house in case the boys return," Nicky told them.

"Ella, you know these woods better than any of us. Which

167

way do you think Calvin would go?" Gabriel asked her.

Ella paced as she thought. Calvin knew these woods, probably as well as she did, but he had never been alone. There were many dangers lurking in the forest that a small child could encounter if he wasn't careful. Granted, she had told Calvin never to wander too close to the edge of the stream, or to climb the hills without a grown-up being there to help. But he might feel it was safe to explore the caves. She couldn't say with complete certainty that he would go there, as they were a good half-hour hike away, but it would be the perfect spot to impress his new friend.

"He might be going toward the caves," she said.

"I know where they are. Jen and I took him there yesterday," Nicky said.

"But you can't say for certain," Gabriel stated.

"No," she agreed. She bit her lip hard while she looked around the forest, searching frantically for a glimpse of the boys.

"Ella, you search the caves. I'll go in the direction of the creek. Gabriel, perhaps you should take that way." Nicky pointed toward the hills that stretched out to their right, down the length of the forest.

Gabriel looked like he was about to argue, but changed his mind, no doubt realizing their efforts would be better spent if they were to split up. He looked at Ella, and then walked over to hold her quickly in his arms. "Don't worry, we'll find them."

"I know we will."

As the two hurried off in different directions, Nicky called out to them, "I know it's tempting to run as you're looking, but keep your sights trained on your surroundings. Search as you walk for any footprints, broken branches, anything to indicate the boys have passed in that direction," he instructed.

Ella gave a quick nod in acknowledgement. She strode off, calling out the boys' names. After ten minutes of walking along a faint trail leading in the direction of the caves, she tried to remain calm. If Calvin had just gone there yesterday, it would make sense he would head that way again, being familiar with the direction. She called out to the boys, and even called to Samson, hoping the animal might bark if he heard her voice. It comforted her slightly to know they must have the big black dog with them since he'd not been in the yard. He would at least keep away any other animals that might happen by.

Thirty minutes later, Ella reached the caves, the three of them carved deeply into the side of a hill. The nearest was set almost twenty feet up from the ground, and from where she stood it appeared unoccupied. "Calvin!" she yelled, though she feared the boys were not there. There hadn't been anything along the path to indicate they had passed this way. She climbed up the hill and peered through the darkness into the depths of the first cave before searching the others. The boys were not inside, and suddenly Ella felt very afraid. She had wasted so much time coming here, and the boys were nowhere to be found.

Quickly she ran back down the pathway she had so carefully followed earlier. Perhaps the boys had returned to the house, or Gabriel or Nicky might have found them, she thought, her steps slowing as she tired. She should have thought to bring the walkie-talkies she had. They'd been one of Calvin's Christmas gifts last year. At first he'd brought them along everywhere they went. Even when he went to the babysitter's house, he'd talked Mrs. MacKenzie into taking them along on their hikes. They were handy as well, since Ella couldn't afford a cell phone anymore. And besides, the service, unless you were right in town, was static at best.

It took her under twenty minutes to return to the backyard. As she crossed through the gate her eyes darted around, hoping to settle upon the boys. But only Jen was in the yard. She had been sitting at the picnic table but rose when she saw her.

"Did you find them?" Jen asked as she rushed up to meet Ella, who was striding toward her.

"No," Ella replied despondently. "I searched the caves, but they weren't there. Gabriel is checking around the hills and Nicky went to the creek."

"Oh."

Ella could tell Jen had been crying. "Maybe one of the guys found them and is bringing them home right now," Ella said, turning her gaze to the back of the yard. She closed her eyes and prayed for the boys to appear. When she opened them, she was amazed to see Gabriel suddenly stepping through the open gate. She didn't waste any time rushing forward to meet him. Jen was right behind her. The look on his face wasn't encouraging, and Ella didn't have to voice the question that was on her mind.

"They weren't at the hills," he told her, seeing she'd had no luck either.

Ella noticed his hands were shaking, and she had no doubt his heart was racing as fast as hers.

"Nicky might have found them," Jen told them hopefully. "Did you know he's an expert tracker?"

"Let's grab some water and head out again," Gabriel said to Ella, ignoring Jen's words.

Ella nodded her head in agreement and ran into the house. She soon returned with two canteens slung over her shoulder, and made sure to grab the walkie-talkies. She walked over and handed one to Gabriel, along with a canteen.

"Good idea," he said, eyeing the radios. "I've noticed I'm lucky to get any kind of signal on my phone unless I'm right in town. If Nicky returns, tell him we've gone back out," Gabriel said to Jen as they headed over toward the gate.

Ella stopped. "We should call the police," she said suddenly. "They could organize a search party. That way we'd cover a lot more ground."

"That's a good idea," Gabriel agreed. "I want to continue searching, but you could call the police and wait for them with Jen."

Ella could see the sense of Gabriel's plan, but it meant that she would have to stay behind to wait for the police. If she had to stand around doing nothing, she wasn't sure she could keep from becoming hysterical. The thought of her baby and Gabriel's child alone in the woods with only a dog to protect them was enough to push her over the edge. If she let herself stop and think, she knew she would break down.

"I...I can't stay here," she said. Tears began to pool in her eyes and her vision blurred.

Gabriel obviously understood her fear. "Ella, you were right to suggest calling the police. If you can't wait for them, then let Jen make the call. Okay?"

"I'll do it, Ella. You go, all right? I can tell them all they need to know," Jen assured her.

Ella nodded her head. "Let's go," she said to Gabriel.

He took her hand, and as Jen hurried off to call the police, they began to walk toward the forest. They had almost reached the fence when Nicky suddenly stepped through the gate. Under each arm he carried a soaking child. Samson barreled through the gate, just as wet as the boys.

Ella and Gabriel froze as they stared at the sight before them. Gabriel was the first to break the spell by shouting for joy as he reached out to take his son. Ella watched as Nicky gently placed Calvin on the ground before her. She sunk to her knees and put her hands out to catch him as he leaped into her arms.

"Sorry, Mommy," he rasped.

His little body was shaking, and Ella wasn't certain if he had a chill from his wet clothing or if he shook from his frightening ordeal. "You're safe now, sweet pea."

Jen, who had heard Gabriel's yell, ran over and leaned down to give Calvin a quick hug. "I'll get some blankets," she told Ella, wiping tears from her eyes as she hurried away.

Ella held Calvin tightly against her to warm him as her eyes looked to Nicky. "Thank you. I don't know how I'll ever repay you."

Nicky smiled. "I owed you one, remember?"

"I take it you found them by the creek?" Gabriel asked him.

"More like *in* the creek."

"What were you doing there?" Ella asked Calvin.

Calvin looked over at Darius, who was being held in his

father's arms. "We wanted to do some ex-plorin'."

Darius had a guilty look on his face. "It...it was my idea," he said quietly. "I saw Samson over by the gate and I opened it. When he ran through I saw how big the forest looked, and I asked Calvin to go exploring. He told me we weren't allowed. But, when I called him chicken...we went."

Ella could see the anger on Gabriel's face. She was upset that Calvin would disregard her warnings so callously. Just because he had been goaded into this little adventure, it wasn't an excuse for what he'd done. She would be sure to give him a long lecture on the importance of heeding her words. But right now, all she wanted to do was hold him.

Jen returned to wrap the boys in blankets. They carried them inside and sat them before the fireplace, where Nicky lit a small blaze. Jen made hot chocolate and the boys cradled the mugs gratefully in their hands while they warmed up. It was then they revealed their story.

"We went into the forest and decided we should follow Samson," Calvin began, pointing at the dog that had joined them to dry himself by the fire. "He must have been thirsty, 'cause he went right to the creek."

"There are some rocks in the water near the shore that Samson jumped onto. We called him, but he wouldn't jump back over. We thought maybe he might be stuck there, or that he was afraid to jump back. We had to go and get him," Darius continued.

"Yeah, but Darius don't jump so good," Calvin informed them.

"You didn't jump so good yourself!" Darius snapped, his face flaming.

"I woulda made it if you hadn't grabbed onto me!" Calvin yelled.

"Would not!"

"Would too!"

"Enough!" snapped Gabriel. "I can't believe you two went off into the woods when you both know how dangerous it is. If Nicky hadn't found you when he did, God only knows what might have happened...." His voice trailed off, and he had to look down at the floor to hide his pained expression.

Ella knew how afraid he'd been. It had been hard for him because he'd had to be strong for the both of them. Now that the boys were safe, he was beginning to let his guard down, and he wasn't prepared for the sudden onslaught of his emotions.

Gabriel looked up at Nicky then. "Thank you," he said, his voice thick with feeling.

Nicky seemed slightly overwhelmed by the gratitude he was receiving. Jen had gushed over him after giving the boys their hot chocolates, telling him over and over how wonderful he was.

"You're welcome, mate," he said.

Ella smiled at Nicky's embarrassed expression. One day, after his own child was born, he would understand why what had happened today had been such an ordeal.

Gabriel left for the cottage twenty minutes later. Darius, still wrapped in his blanket, bid a shy farewell to Ella. "It was nice to meet you," he told her. "I'm sorry I got lost in your forest."

Ella gave him a quick hug goodbye. "I'm sorry too, Darius. But it was very nice to meet you."

"I'll call you later," Gabriel said.

Ella made Calvin a grilled cheese sandwich for lunch, and then, despite his objections, tucked him into his bed for an afternoon nap. Nicky had left soon after Gabriel, and now that she and Jen were alone, Ella knew it was a good time to broach the subject of Jen's condition. "I've got something for you," she told her.

Jen, who was sitting at the kitchen table, looked at her curiously. Ella rose and walked over to the fridge to grab the pregnancy test she'd picked up that morning. She placed it on the kitchen table before Jen, who stared at it.

"I can't...," she whispered with fright.

Ella sat back down beside her. "Yes, you can." Jen's face had become pale. Ella knew it was hard for her, but it had to be done. Jen had to know if she was carrying Nicky's child. She watched as Jen picked up the test and walked slowly toward the bathroom, her head hanging low, as though she were headed to her own execution.

She returned ten minutes later.

"Well?" Ella prodded.

Jen went over to the table and sat down. She handed the test to Ella and turned her head away. "I don't know yet. It says it could take up to fifteen minutes to get a result."

Ella peered at the test and tried to decipher what the outcome was. "What does it mean if there's a line showing in both of the little windows?" she asked.

Jen slapped her hand to her forehead. "It means I'm gonna be changing diapers," she said in despair.

~*~

"This is the biggest one I've ever seen!" Darius said

excitedly from the back of the cave. He had run inside with Calvin after Ella had given them the all clear.

"I told ya!" yelled Calvin, his voice echoing around the walls.

While the boys explored, Gabriel remained at the entrance with Ella, finally grabbing a moment to themselves. It was Sunday afternoon. He had called her last night after putting Darius to bed. Ella had just tucked Calvin in, so she was content to curl up on the couch and talk. They'd discussed what had happened that morning. Gabriel was upset, but his time with Darius was short so he was hesitant to punish him. Ella had reassured him that a verbal reprimand was enough, due to the circumstances. He'd offered to pick them up after church so they could all go out to lunch, and she'd agreed.

Ella had mentioned the vacant store to Gabriel, revealing how she had always dreamed of owning a bookstore. Gabriel had listened and been very supportive of her ideas. Feeling inspired after she hung up the phone, Ella began to put her plans down onto paper. On Monday, she would call the bank and set up a meeting to present her plan to Mr. Bentley.

"Come on up," Calvin shouted to Darius.

Darius eyed the ledge high over his head with trepidation. "It's awfully high."

"What's the matter? Ya chicken or something?" Calvin laughed gleefully.

"Calvin!" Ella scolded, stalking into the cave toward him. "Have you forgotten our discussion from last night? Do we need to sit down and have another talk?"

"No," Calvin quickly assured her.

Darius waited until Ella had turned her head away before

he stuck his tongue out at Calvin, and then climbed up to join him on the ledge.

"Hello, in there!" yelled a voice suddenly from the large opening of the cave.

"Is that you, Nicky?" Calvin yelled back excitedly.

"You in there, little mate?" Nicky called, squinting into the darkness.

"Back here, on the ledge."

Nicky walked into the cave with Jen clinging to his arm. "I thought I might find you here," he said, with a smile to Ella and Gabriel as he came up beside them.

Gabriel reached out to slap Nicky on the back in a friendly greeting, the animosity between them now completely gone. "This cave is incredible, don't you think?"

"Yeah, Jen's only dragged me here half a dozen times already."

While the men talked, Ella discreetly led Jen off just outside the entranceway to the cave.

"Have you told him yet?" she asked her cousin quietly.

Jen looked uncomfortable and, leaning down to pick up a small stone, turned it over in the palm of her hand. "No," she replied, her eyes flashing over at Nicky.

Ella knew this was difficult for her, but she had told her last night ignoring the situation wouldn't make it go away. She sighed when Jen whispered she was waiting for just the right moment. Her cousin strode toward Nicky then and Ella watched her go, wishing there was something she could do to make things easier for her.

They took the boys to Mom's Restaurant for dinner that evening. Darius ordered a huge hamburger, fries, and a shake.

Calvin ordered the same, and when their meals arrived, they quickly dug in, making it a race to see who could clean their plate first.

"Slow down, Calvin. You'll make yourself sick," Ella scolded when she saw him jam a handful of fries into his mouth.

"You too," Gabriel said to Darius, whose cheeks were puffed out like a chipmunk's.

Ella was happy the two boys got along so well, except of course for the never ending competition they had going on. They almost acted as though they were brothers, she thought.

When Monday morning arrived, Ella couldn't help but feel a touch of trepidation. Once again she was sitting outside of Mr. Bentley's office. Gabriel had gone over her notes with her last night after dinner. Jen and Nicky had even gotten involved and offered up their own comments and suggestions.

Ella had summoned her strength and called the bank first thing in the morning. They told her to come over at ten o'clock. She'd packed up notes and left Calvin in Jen's capable hands.

Amazingly, Mr. Bentley was all for her idea. He wrote up an agreement with her on the spot, and despite Ella's earlier fears, she left the bank glowing with pride. She'd done it! She had secured a business line of credit to pay rent on her store, and had extra to spare for start-up costs and renovations.

She quickly headed to the realty company that held the rental on the vacant store. After a deal was struck and more papers signed, she handed over a check for first and last month's rent. Soon holding the store key in her hand, Ella was amazed at how quickly and smoothly things had gone.

The contributing factor, no doubt, was that she was quite well known in this small town, and most everyone knew what had happened to the library. Her new landlord was all for Ella's idea to open a bookstore coffee shop, believing it would been an asset to Caverly.

Ella went home and picked up Calvin, and asked Jen and Nicky to drive over to meet her at the store.

"Mommy, is this our house now?" Calvin asked, looking around in awe.

Ella laughed. "No, sweetheart, this is going to be Mommy's new store."

"What kinda store?"

"A bookstore, along with a coffee shop."

Calvin scrunched up his face. "Why can't ya open a bakery, like the one that was here before?"

Ella knelt down before him. "Do you remember that the library burned down? All the people in town don't have a place to get books now, and they won't for months and months. But we have lots of books in our basement, and Mommy can order new books and magazines. If we install some shelves and put out our books, then people can have something to read again."

"I think they'd rather have somethin' to eat."

"Well, I think it's a wonderful idea," Jen gushed, making Ella feel excited again about her new endeavor.

"So do I," Nicky said, looking pointedly at Calvin.

Calvin signed loudly. "Oh, all right. If you think it's a good idea then so do I," he said, looking at Nicky. "But I still wish we was openin' a bakery."

The rest of the week sped by with taking Darius to all the

many sights to be seen in Caverly. Calvin enjoyed playing the guide by day, while in the evenings, Darius told stories about the many exciting places he'd seen while accompanying his mother on tours to foreign lands. Ella's mornings were spent loading up her car with boxes of books and taking them over to the store. Nicky had helped her to order shelving units, and when they arrived he and Gabriel assembled and then drilled them to the walls while the boys played board games in the back of the store. Ella's time was divided between Gabriel and the boys and being at the store. She'd fallen into bed each night feeling exhausted, but she was ecstatically happy. If everything went according to plan, she would be ready to open her doors to the public by the end of the summer.

She'd told Cate and Sarah about her plans, and they'd rolled up their sleeves and pitched in to help her clean up and haul boxes. This felt right, Ella thought, eyeing their progress with pride.

Not only was this undertaking something good for the town, it was good for her and her family too. She was taking charge of her life, no longer awaiting fate and chance to decide her life's course.

All too soon, Saturday arrived and it was time for Sonia to pick up Darius. Ella drove over early in the morning so that she and Calvin could say their goodbyes. She felt a lump form in her throat when the two boys shook hands before Darius hugged her.

"Do you want to stay and meet Sonia?" Gabriel asked her.

"No, thanks. I need to go online and check out popular flavored coffees and suppliers. I'm also keeping an eye out for deals on little tables and big comfy chairs. I think I'll drive by some garage sales in town as well." She silently called herself a coward as she drove away, realizing she was still very embarrassed and ashamed of her jealous behavior last week.

Jen had headed out early with Nicky this morning, and assured Ella that today would definitely be the day she revealed her condition. After gathering up two more boxes of books at garage sales, Ella headed home. She wondered how Jen was doing at breaking her news to Nicky. When she pulled into her driveway, she could see Nicky's car just pulling out. She waved as he drove past her, and wasn't surprised he spared her only a brief nod. Jen must have told him, she thought as she entered the house with Calvin.

She poured Calvin a glass of milk and went in search of her cousin. As expected, she found her curled up on her bed, crying her eyes out. Ella sat on the side of the bed and took Jen's hand to comfort her.

"It's all right, Jen," she soothed. "You had to expect him to take it hard."

Jen sniffled as she looked up at Ella. "I can't believe he acted the way he did," she said. "I never would have thought he'd...."

Ella was concerned by the look on Jen's face. "What did he do? He didn't break things off with you, did he?" she demanded.

"No. It isn't that. He...he wants to marry me!"

The next week passed with Ella only receiving the odd phone call from Gabriel. She hadn't seen him since last Saturday, but he had called and warned her early in the week that he wanted to accomplish something on his novel. While Darius had been with him, he hadn't had time to do anything more than jot down a few sentences, and he'd been anxious to get back to work. Ella was glad he was so enthusiastic about this new story of his. She didn't mind not seeing him considering all the work she had to do at the store, not to mention the drama she was caught up in at home.

Ever since Nicky had discovered he was going to be a father, he had spent each day determined to try every outlandish stunt he could think of. He jumped out of a plane three more times, although this time he made sure his jumps were into empty fields. He'd rock climbed Eagle's Landing, gone scuba diving in five different lakes, and white water rafted over the side of a waterfall, all in the span of a week. Jen explained the reasoning for his actions was that he was living each day to the fullest up until the time when he must settle down for good. He hadn't made it known just yet when he had decided that day would be, since Jen couldn't get him to commit to a wedding date. He had spent a small fortune on an engagement ring, though, which he'd rushed out to buy the same day he'd heard the happy news.

Ella had to admit, Nicky did seem very excited about the idea of becoming a father. He would stop by the house and talk about the baby, then rush off to climb up a rock face, while Jen would stomp off to her room. Ella had told Jen that although she was pregnant, it didn't mean she had to accept Nicky's proposal. She remembered how Gabriel had told her he'd married Sonia for just that reason, and their marriage had ultimately failed because of it. She was worried Jen might be making the same mistake.

But then, she would look outside her window at night, and see the two of them together. Nicky would return from one of his adventures, and he and Jen would sit outside under the moonlight, holding each other. Ella recalled how devastated Jen had been when Nicky wasn't in her life. They loved each other, she could see it in their faces. The way Nicky looked at Jen reminded Ella of how Joe used to look at her, and deep down inside she knew they would be all right. It didn't surprise her that on Sunday, when Nicky arrived to take Jen to church, they told Ella they'd decided to go home in a few days to break their news to Jen's parents. Ella, though worried about how her aunt and uncle would respond to their announcement, couldn't help but agree with the young couple.

Monday evening everyone relaxed outside after finishing dinner. Calvin threw a ball for Samson to retrieve while Jen and Nicky cuddled at the picnic table. Ella was just heading outside with coffee when the phone rang. She set the tray of hot mugs aside while she answered it.

"Ella, I'm sorry to bother you with this, but the pump seems to be acting up again."

It was Gabriel, and she couldn't deny she was pleased to hear from him. She told him she'd be right over, and went outside to ask her cousin to watch Calvin for her.

"I wanna go with you, Mommy," Calvin whined. "I haven't seen Gab-real all week."

Ella felt badly that Calvin missed Gabriel, but she knew fixing the pump might take her a while and she didn't want him up too late. She also had to admit to herself that she had a very selfish desire to spend some time alone with him. "Not tonight, Calvin. I'll ask Gabriel if we can bring lunch over to the cottage tomorrow, and maybe we could have a picnic, all right?" she asked him, knowing he would enjoy that.

"Okay," he said grudgingly before running off to toss the ball again.

Ella turned to Jen. "Are you sure you don't mind watching him?"

"Of course, I don't mind."

Nicky reached around Jen to playfully rub her belly. "We need the practice," he winked.

Fifteen minutes later Ella was pulling up outside of her uncle's cottage. Gabriel came out to the back porch to meet her as she climbed out of her car.

"Hi," he said as she strolled toward him.

"Hi, yourself." She had missed him this week, and faintly wondered what would happen when the summer ended and he left for good. She pushed those thoughts away for now, not liking the sudden empty feeling in the pit of her stomach.

"The pump sounded like it did the last time," he told her. "And I didn't really see how you fixed it."

"Can you grab me a bucket and fill it in the lake?" she asked him as she started around the side of the cottage.

Gabriel went inside and returned with the bucket. After filling it, he knelt down and peered at Ella underneath the cottage. He passed the bucket to her and then looked at his watch.

"Do you think you'll be all right to do this alone if I were to leave?" he asked her.

Ella was surprised at his question. "You need to go somewhere?"

"Yes. That lake you took me to before."

"Bethower?"

"That's the one."

"Why do you need to go there now? It takes a while to get there, and you might not get back until after dark," Ella told him, not liking the idea.

"I want to photograph the sunset at the lake," he explained.

Ella noticed he had his camera bag beside him. "Why don't you wait for me to take you?" she suggested.

"You have your hands full here, and I had my heart set on going now," he told her. "I'm plotting the next scene of my book, and I really need to take the pictures tonight."

Ella remembered that Gabriel had told her he needed to experience certain aspects of his stories as he wrote them to make them as real as possible.

"I understand," she told him. "But I'm just worried you won't be able to find your way back. The trail is difficult to follow, even in the light."

"I have a flashlight," he said, smiling over her worried tone. "And I also have Calvin's map." He patted the breast pocket of his shirt and gave her a wink.

Ella couldn't help but laugh. "Well then, I guess you'll be all right."

"I'll take the paddle boat across the lake. That way I can rest my flashlight on the seat beside me on the way back home," he told her.

Ella wondered how well this plan of his would work out when daylight disappeared and he was alone with only Calvin's map and a flashlight on an overgrown trail. But judging by the look on his face, she knew it would be useless to argue with him.

"Good luck to you then," she said. "And Gabriel…please

185

be careful."

"I will," he said as he picked up his bag and walked toward the dock.

Ella set to work on the pump, knowing she would have a long tense evening ahead of her waiting for Gabriel to return.

Chapter Twelve

Ella climbed out from underneath the cottage to stretch her legs. It had taken her almost thirty minutes to prime the pump, and her leg muscles were stiff and painful. She leaned her shoulder against the solid wood of the cottage as she balanced from foot to foot, trying to restore feeling to her limbs. When she was finally able to support her own weight, she started to walk slowly around to the back door. She gazed down toward the lake, almost tempted to walk out onto the dock. She checked her watch and noticed how much time had passed since Gabriel had left, and felt certain he should be well on his way by now.

A sudden cool breeze blew past her, and Ella shivered as she turned her head up toward the sky. While she'd been under the cottage she'd not seen the thick dark clouds that were moving in overhead at alarming speed. Hopefully, she thought, hurrying out to the dock, Gabriel had noticed them and was now making his way back to the cottage. But as she stared far off across the surface of the water, she saw he was nowhere in sight. Uncertain of what she should do, but only for an instant, she made up her mind. If a storm broke, as it looked like it was about to, then Gabriel wouldn't be able to come across the lake to get back. It wasn't safe. No, she needed to find him and bring him home on the trail around the lake. It was a much longer route than the one she'd shown him, but it would be safer during a storm.

Ella jogged up to the cottage and went directly inside to the bedroom with a phone. She quickly called Jen and let her know what had happened and what she intended to do. Then she grabbed one of her aunt's old jackets out of a trunk and picked up a flashlight from under the kitchen sink. She filled a canteen with water and slung it over her shoulder before heading back toward the lake. She'd have to go across in the canoe, but it would be much faster than hiking up the trail she intended to take to get back, for time was of the essence now. If she went the other way, she could miss Gabriel completely.

She climbed into the boat, put the canteen at her feet, and began stroking across the water, which was becoming rougher since the wind had picked up. Overhead the sky was almost black with threatening clouds. Hopefully the rain would hold off long enough for her to find Gabriel, she thought. Surely he would notice the approaching storm—it would hamper his chances of catching a beautiful sunset on camera.

It took her almost fifteen minutes to pull up beside the paddleboat tied at the rock face where the trail to Bethower Lake began. When they had picnicked in this spot it had been tranquil and undisturbed, but now the wind was whipping through the trees and scattering pine needles and dead crinkled leaves. Ella tugged the canoe up out of the water as far as she could and secured the rope to a sturdy tree. She swung her canteen over her shoulder and pulled the hood of her aunt's jacket over her head. Heavy rain began to fall as she stepped onto the trail leading into the dark forest.

Head down, body bent forward, and arms wrapped around her sides for warmth, she fought the biting wind. Rain stung her cheeks whenever she raised her head to gauge her progress, forcing her to keep her eyes downcast at her sodden shoes. She kept to the trail, mostly by instinct and years of familiarity. From quick peeks, she knew her destination was getting close. Suddenly she plowed into a brick wall, and found herself falling backward before sitting stunned upon the ground, her jeans quickly became drenched with the wet mud beneath her. She squinted upward, confused over what on earth she had run into, and assumed she'd misgauged her steps and walked into one of the trees. If so, then this must be an enchanted forest, she mused, for it suddenly reached out its limbs and gently latched onto her arms to lift her to her feet.

"Ella! Are you all right?" shouted the tree, its voice all but snatched away by the wind. Ella peered more closely, and as her head began to clear, she noticed it was no tree that held her, but Gabriel, and he, like her, was soaked to the skin.

"I'm okay," she yelled, though their faces were but inches apart.

Gabriel tried to frown at her. "What were you thinking coming here in this weather?"

"I was worried about you coming back across the lake in the storm."

Gabriel led her slightly off the trail and leaned his back against a thick trunk of a tree, giving them a slight reprieve from the wind. He pulled her closer to his chest, wrapping his arms around her to share his warmth. Ella was surprised he was, in fact, still quite warm despite his wet clothes.

"We need to find shelter," he said, his lips next to her ear. "We can't risk going across the lake now."

Ella arched her head to look him in the eye. "There's another way back. That's why I came, so I could lead you home."

"Another way?"

She stepped out of the comfort of his arms, knowing they had to move quickly if they were going to make it home before completely losing what little daylight they had left. "We have to go now," she insisted when Gabriel reached out and held tightly to her hand.

Clearly seeing the urgency in her look, he walked with her to the trail and allowed her to lead him back the way he had just come from. He tried to keep her behind him so she might be shielded from the brunt of the storm, but Ella pushed his hands from her so that she could walk up beside him.

"I can't show you where to go if I can't see the trail," she yelled, as he again tried to force her back.

Gabriel finally relented and allowed her to walk beside him, but pulled her close to his side and put a protective arm around her waist.

They continued on, not speaking to each other so that they may save their strength to fight the wind and rain. The mud on the trail hampered their journey, sucking at their shoes and weighing them down with a thick mucky coating. Darkness was descending rapidly. As they passed by Bethower Lake Ella knew they still had a good hour-long walk ahead of them. They would never make it, she thought. She stopped suddenly, forcing Gabriel to turn toward her.

"What is it?" he hollered, anxious with the delay.

"We aren't going to make it back before it's too dark to see," she yelled. "I have a flashlight, but the storm is getting worse. I know where there's a cabin. It's close by, and I think we should take shelter there."

Gabriel appeared undecided for a moment before he nodded his head in agreement. Ella needed no further encouragement—she broke from the trail and headed into the forest. She could barely make out a high slope in the distance, but she knew the cabin was just at the base of it. She led them on a winding path over fallen logs and slippery moss-covered rocks toward the cabin, which she could now see quite easily through the slight cover the trees offered.

"There!" Ella pointed, and allowed Gabriel to take the lead. It was moments later when they finally stood outside the cabin and Gabriel pushed the rickety old door open and stepped inside. He shined his flashlight around the single room of the tiny dwelling, making sure it was free from any wild creatures, before pulling her in beside him.

Ella turned and closed the door, shutting out the storm. She pulled out her own flashlight and shined the light up at the ceiling. Except for a few small leaks splashing rain onto the wooden floor below, the roof appeared quite sturdy. Shining her light around the rest of the place, she noticed it was exactly as she remembered. The kitchen area was as dusty as ever, and a rickety table and chairs still sat beneath the only window. A small wooden framed bed with a thin mattress was tucked into the corner, complete with a tattered old quilt tucked neatly around it. Best of all was the ancient fireplace. Nothing had changed.

Thankfully there was a stack of dry wood, and Gabriel wasted no time starting a warm crackling fire to take the chill from the air. He then fetched one of the two chairs and placed it close by the fire before helping Ella to peel off her wet jacket. Once he had it draped across the back of the chair, he began removing his own sodden clothes. Soon he stood before the fire wearing only his boxer shorts, which were wet and molded to his muscular thighs, not leaving much to the imagination.

Ella stood before the flames stretching out her hands to feel the heat, trying to keep her eyes focused on the fire. She knew she should do as Gabriel had done and shed her own clothing, but her modesty kept her from doing so. As she stood there feeling chilled and miserable, Gabriel left the fire for a moment before returning with the other chair, then he grabbed the old quilt from the bed. He held it up before her and she smiled at him gratefully. It didn't take her long to remove her own wet clothes before wrapping herself in the warmth of the quilt.

She felt awkward standing beside Gabriel wearing just a quilt over her bra and panties with him in only his boxers. Then she began to feel guilty that she was warm while he was shivering. The guilt grew inside of her until she could no longer stand it. Her hand, still holding tightly to the corner of the quilt, stretched out across his back to rest on his shoulder. Gabriel stepped closer toward her and took the corner of the quilt from her hand, wrapping it more snugly around his body. It was Ella's turn to shiver, and she wondered if it was from the chill of Gabriel's skin or from the sudden close proximity of their bodies. Their skin brushed intimately, and Ella laughed lightly to cover the embarrassment she felt.

"Better?" she asked him, referring to the heat she now felt radiating from his chest.

Gabriel's look was also heated as he cleared his throat before he answered her. "Ah, yes, thank you. Much better."

Lightning suddenly lit up the room, and was soon followed by a huge clap of thunder. The sound of the rain on the roof was fierce, and Ella mouthed a silent prayer that the cabin would hold up under the relentless pressure. The wind howled outside so loudly that every word they spoke to one another had to be in raised voices, making any conversation an effort. They remained before the fire for what seemed like hours, listening to the storm, before Ella began to feel her legs grow tired from the position.

"Do you mind if we sit down?" she asked.

He looked at her from his great height, then turned his gaze to the floor beneath them. Ella also looked toward her toes that peeked out from under the quilt, and could barely make out the grimy wooden planks that felt chilled and hard. Sitting on the dirty floor didn't seem like an option, so she didn't object when Gabriel led her over toward the tiny bed. He sat down on the thin mattress, and Ella quickly sat down beside him.

"It's late," he said. "Perhaps we should just try and sleep, and we can get out of here in the morning when our clothes are dry."

"Yes," she agreed, hoping the storm would be over by then.

Gabriel looked at her regretfully. "This is my fault. If I'd come back as soon as I noticed the sky blackening we could have avoided all this."

"Don't worry about it. It happened so fast, there wasn't really any time. Besides, things turn out the way they do for a reason." It was something she had told herself many times over the years.

Gabriel lay back on the mattress and Ella curled up on her side close by him. It didn't take long for her to give in to exhaustion and fall into a deep sleep. As she slept, she dreamed. Dreamed of the feel of Gabriel's hands upon her skin and running through her hair. His lips were warm, and she could feel them on her shoulder and then her neck before they kissed their way up to join passionately with her own. Ella awoke suddenly when she felt the weight of Gabriel's body slide over her, and she realized this was not just a dream she was having. Her arms were wrapped around Gabriel's broad shoulders, and her fingers were entwined deeply in the thickness of his mane. She gasped suddenly when she felt the hardness of him pressing suggestively against her hip, and she shoved at him with all her might.

"What do you think you're doing? Get off me!"

Gabriel stared at her through half open eyes still lit with the heat of passion. It appeared he too had been caught up in the rapture of dreams, as his eyes suddenly flew open and he stared around himself as if he wasn't certain where he was.

"Ella?" he croaked. "I thought.... I thought I was dreaming."

SEND ME AN ANGEL

She could tell by the look on his face that he wasn't pretending, and he had indeed been acting out what they had both thought was a harmless fantasy. She climbed from the bed as soon as she was free of his weight and pulled the quilt up around herself. Gabriel gave a slight shiver, but Ella was hesitant about rejoining him. It was obvious they shared a mutual attraction for one another, and lying so close could tempt them into doing something they may regret. She also couldn't deny the fact that the summer was coming to an end. If she gave into her feelings and let Gabriel make love to her, she wasn't sure she could let him go so easily. She knew she was being overly cautious, considering how sorry Gabriel appeared to be. He would now surely keep his hands to himself. Or was it herself and her own body she was more concerned about, she wondered? She couldn't deny she had been kissing Gabriel with ardent desire, and a desperate need to join with him.

Gabriel held out his hand in a silent invitation to come back to him, and Ella sighed before she sunk back down beside him onto the bed. He cautiously pulled the quilt back around the both of them while trying to keep their bodies from touching. He then peered at Ella through the dimness of the light and smiled.

"It wouldn't be so bad, you know," he said to her, his voice playful.

Ella couldn't help but smile back at him. "I know, that's why we can't."

"Afraid we might never leave this leaky little cabin again?"

"No. I'm afraid of what will happen when we do leave,"

she said quietly before rolling onto her side away from him.

They awoke the next morning wrapped tightly in each other's arms. Sometime in the night the fire had gone out and the room had grown cold. Mercifully, the rain had stopped and the wind had died down to a slight breeze that blew over the forest, causing last night's raindrops to fall from the trees. They dressed in silence and left the cabin as they had found it, although Ella knew she would never look at the old place quite the same way again.

"We don't need to worry about taking the long way around the lake now," she said, as they reached the trail they'd journeyed down last night. "We'll probably have a lot of bailing to do with the boats though, considering I couldn't turn them over by myself." She laughed after speaking, trying to lighten the tension in the air she'd felt since leaving the cabin. Gabriel had hardly spoken two words to her since rising this morning, and Ella couldn't understand what was bothering him. Perhaps he was annoyed she hadn't succumbed to his considerable charms last night? Or perhaps, it just might be that he was regretting what had happened between them, she thought, considering the downcast look on his face.

When they reached the boats, she helped him tip them up to get the water out before they crossed back over the lake to the cottage. When they reached the shore, she declined his polite invitation to join him inside for breakfast, giving the excuse that Calvin and Jen would be worried about her. They awkwardly embraced each other, as though they had suddenly become uncomfortable in each other's presence.

When she returned home, Jen rushed outside to greet her with Calvin fast behind. His little legs quickly overtook Jen, and he was standing in front of Ella as she climbed out of her car.

"Mommy, did you find Gab-real? Were you lost in the storm all night?"

Jen looked at Ella over Calvin's head and gave her an apologetic smile. "He wouldn't go to bed until I told him what was going on."

"It's all right. Let's go inside and have some breakfast, and I'll tell you everything." Well, perhaps not *everything*, she thought.

They ate eggs and toast and Ella had two cups of strong coffee. She filled them in on how her night had gone, and avoided the questioning glances Jen threw at her when she spoke about having to sleep in the old cabin. Calvin's endless stream of questions was broken off when the dog gained his attention by scratching frantically at the back door.

"I'd better take Samson out," he sighed while getting to his feet.

"That sounds like a good idea," Ella agreed.

After Calvin went outside and the screen door clicked shut behind him, Ella was certain Jen was going to give her the third degree about spending the night alone with Gabriel. She was relieved when Jen instead informed her that she'd decided she was going to leave today with Nicky to go home.

"I think it's time to face the music."

Ella didn't have to ask her what that remark meant. Considering Katherine's behavior and Jen's obvious trepidation, she could well imagine how her family felt about Nicky. She didn't have to wonder how they would take the news that Jen was going to have a little bundle of joy with the man.

Two hours later Ella was waving goodbye to her cousin and her fiancé. After dinner, she was surprised when Gabriel called. He asked if she could arrange to get a sitter for Calvin and meet him down at her store. Ella was hesitant about meeting him considering the tone of his voice and the way he'd acted this morning, but twenty minutes later she stood before the store after arranging with Sarah to come and sit with Calvin.

Gabriel looked around at the neatly stacked shelves when he walked inside the store. "You've made a lot of progress. Think you'll be ready to open up shop soon?"

"Yes, maybe even sooner than I'd planned." She knelt down before a box of books and began piling them on the floor beside her. Most of the boxes she'd arranged by fiction and non-fiction when she packed them away, but she still liked to look at each one to familiarize herself with her inventory. Eventually she would alphabetize the fiction shelves by author, and non-fiction would be arranged by the Dewey Decimal System. But right now she just wanted to get them put out onto the shelves to see how many she actually had.

Gabriel paced back and forth while Ella tried to concentrate on her task. She knew he had something on his mind and that he wanted to talk, but she wasn't sure she was ready to hear what he had to say.

"What's wrong Gabriel?" she asked, not being able to stand the tension any longer.

He let out a sigh. "Am I that obvious?"

She couldn't help but smile at him. "I won't bite, you know."

"I know. I'm sorry." He stepped around the pile of books she was forming to kneel down at the box beside her. "I've just felt a little off since this morning, since we spent the night together."

Blushing, she ducked her head from his sight. "You make it sound so sinister. It's not like anything happened."

"I know, but something almost did happen," he reminded her.

"Let's not get all worked up about it, okay? Let's just put it behind us and not waste what time we have left this summer worrying about *what if*."

Gabriel laughed all of a sudden, as if a huge weight had been lifted from his shoulders. Ella wondered if he had been afraid that she was going to tell him he'd ruined her reputation and insist he do right by her. She grinned back at him, then reached into the box to pull out another novel. She paused suddenly when she saw the title of the book she held. It was a classic, one of her favorites, something Joe had bought for her. She opened the cover and saw his handwriting on the page. *To my darling Ella. I love you with all my heart. Always, Joe.*

She closed the book and set it aside, but not with the others. She would never sell this book, not when it had been a gift to her from her beloved Joe. A wave of sadness passed over her for a moment, but she quickly brushed it aside. She reached inside the box to pull out another book when Gabriel, who was going through the box beside her, got her attention.

"Hey, what's this?" he asked, holding a black wooden box in his hands.

Ella froze when she saw it. It had been so long since she'd seen it that she thought she'd lost it for good. Cautiously she took the box from Gabriel and placed it on the floor beside her. She lifted the lid and felt a lump form in her throat when she saw the contents. Inside the box were dozens of old love letters and cards sent to her from Joe when they had been dating.

"What is it, Ella?" Gabriel asked when he noticed her eyes begin to fill with tears. "What's wrong?"

Ella closed the lid and picked up the box. She stood up and cautiously made her way to the opposite side of the room, suddenly anxious to put space between herself and Gabriel. "They're letters...from Joe."

"Oh," he said simply, smiling tightly then looking away from her.

Ella watched the expression on his face. He'd obviously noticed the strong effect the mementos of Joe were having on her, and she could see that he was upset because of it. And because he was upset, she suddenly felt angry with him.

"What's the matter with you?" she snapped suddenly. "Aren't I allowed to mourn my husband? Is there something wrong with that? Just a few minutes ago you looked as though you'd been given a reprieve from the guillotine when I told you not to worry about what happened between us at the cabin. It's not as though you want me, but it seems like I can't want anyone else. What's wrong, does it hurt your masculine pride that I still miss my husband? That you haven't been able to wipe his memory from my mind with your very presence?"

Gabriel rose to his feet. "Hold on there a minute! Things were fine between us just a moment ago, and now, all of a sudden, because you find some old love letters, you're treating me like I'm a jerk."

"Well, maybe you are. You think you can just cruise into my life, and my son's, and make us care about you, and then just walk away when you're finished with us. We're not toys, Gabriel, we're human beings. We have feelings, you know."

Gabriel ran a hand through his hair in agitation. "Ella, look, obviously you're upset. You're not thinking clearly. I should leave and give you some time alone."

"Yes, that's a good idea. I think you should leave me alone. And my son too. We've suffered enough loss, and I don't think we're up to losing someone else."

"Stop saying that you're losing me."

"Well, I will lose you. After the summer's over, you'll go home and not look back."

Gabriel looked at her angrily. "You think I'm that callous? You think you and Calvin mean so little to me that I could just go home and forget about you both?"

"Yes!" Ella said, wanting very much for him to leave. "Well, my son and I don't need you either, Gabriel."

"Fine!" He got up and brushed past her to storm out the door.

Ella didn't try to stop him, no matter how much the pain in her heart was hurting her.

That evening, after she returned home and said goodbye to Sarah, she received a call from Jen. Despite the disappointment plaguing her own life, she was happy and relieved to hear things were going well for her cousin.

"I can't believe how Mom and Dad reacted when I told them Nicky and I were going to get married," Jen gushed. "They actually admitted they had been wrong about him. They said they could tell by the change in me it was obvious

201

how happy he makes me. I guess I was pretty glum after we broke up."

No, really? "That's great," Ella told her, trying to force her voice to sound excited.

"They didn't even get mad when I told them about the baby. Mom actually cried, and said she was finally going to get to be a grandmother. Even Katherine wished me well. I think she's finally reconciled herself to the idea, especially now that she's going to be an auntie."

"I'm really happy for you, Jen."

When Ella awoke the next morning, she felt terrible. What had happened between her and Gabriel last night played itself out in her mind like a nightmare. Had she really said all those awful things to him? It was as though seeing the letters from Joe had been a reminder that she was about to suffer another loss in her life. When Gabriel left she would once again be alone. The pain had been sudden and sharp. She'd been angry and hurt, and she'd wanted to lash out and cause pain to someone else. Unfortunately, Gabriel had been a convenient target. She cringed when she recalled how she'd attacked him with her nasty words. She'd been intentionally cruel, and now she regretted it deeply. She had to apologize to him. Even if he never wanted to see her again, she had to let him know how sorry she was.

Ella drove as fast as she dared down the road out of town. She had dropped Calvin off ten minutes earlier at Sarah's house, and headed straight for her uncle's cottage to talk to Gabriel. She was forced to slow down when she turned the car onto the narrow dirt road that led to the lake. She went over her apology again and again in her mind as she drove.

When she at last pulled up in front of the cottage she saw that his car wasn't there. She also noticed all of the curtains were drawn, and in that moment, she knew he hadn't simply taken a trip into town. He was gone. Gone for good and out of her life, just as she had ordered him.

After she left her uncle's cottage she picked up Calvin and went home. She spent the rest of the day trying to distract herself from thoughts of Gabriel, and avoiding Calvin's questions whenever he had asked about him. Finally the long day was over and Ella curled up on her bed. She tried to sleep, but spent most of the night tossing and turning.

The next morning, she was awoken by the shrill of the telephone. It was Aunt Joan, and she informed her she'd been able to secure the church in Caverly for Jen's wedding. The only problem was it had to be the following Saturday, which hadn't left much time for preparations. Most of the arrangements would have to be taken care of in Caverly.

The weekend and most of the following week flew by with a flurry of activity. Her aunt and uncle, and Katherine and Jen, had arrived in town that Saturday afternoon to prepare for the pending nuptials. Nicky had taken up temporary residence in a nearby motel. Jen had arrived with a wedding gown, but there were still flowers to buy and invitations to hand deliver to their friends around Caverly. Not to mention the food that needed to be prepared for the reception afterward, which was to be held in Ella's backyard. A large canopy was erected over the patio in case the weather decided to be uncooperative.

Though Ella was completely caught up in the excitement, and exhausted by the end of each day, she still longed for Gabriel. Surrounded by her family, she could keep her thoughts focused on the wedding. But at night, when she was alone in her room, her thoughts turned to moments spent with him. She couldn't get the image out of her mind of the look on his face when she had told him she and Calvin didn't need him.

It was her guilt and fear that made her act the way she had. The guilt of being unfaithful to Joe's memory, and her fear of losing someone she loved.

But she was feeling the pain of loss right now, she admitted to herself, and she had only herself to blame. She hadn't given Gabriel the chance to tell her what he was planning, she had only just assumed that he would leave her at the end of summer. If she hadn't lashed out at him, perhaps things would be different right now. Maybe he would be here with her helping to plan Jen's wedding, instead of having left town before he intended to. It was already Thursday evening, and nothing short of a miracle would bring him back to her now.

Ella sat at the picnic table outside and watched the sun begin to disappear behind the line of trees. The house was quiet tonight. Calvin had been put to bed early after enjoying an exciting day spent exploring with Nicky. Nicky's parents had arrived in Caverly in the late afternoon, and had joined Jen and her parents for dinner in town. Katherine had gone out with Sarah and Cate, so she and Calvin had spent a quiet evening at home.

While she needed a break from the constant chaos surrounding her every waking moment since her family's arrival, the sudden quiet was cold comfort. In two short days Jen would be married. Nicky had stormed back into her cousin's life with a vengeance, because he had known deep down they were meant to be together. Despite all odds against them, the couple had prevailed and emerged triumphant. They were an inspiration to Ella. A reminder of how love can conquer all.

She suddenly remembered all the wonderful things that had happened in her life recently, and how she too had defied the odds. Things like following her dream to open a bookstore, and securing a future for her and her son. Overcoming her fear of allowing a man to get close to her again. And, she had fallen in love. It was because of her love for Gabriel that she had found the strength to get past the barriers in her life. Now she would use that strength to reclaim what she'd lost. She would go after him.

Tomorrow, she decided, she would get into her car, drive to Toronto, and seek out Gabriel Stolks. She'd find him, she was certain, for how hard could it be to track down a famous author? It was true he probably wouldn't see her, but she was determined. Just like Nicky wouldn't take no for an answer, she would be the same. She would make him hear her out. Even if he didn't accept her apology, she would know that she'd done everything in her power to make things right. She just hoped it would be enough.

She was so caught up with her plans that she failed to hear the approaching footsteps coming across the yard until they were directly behind her.

"Ella?"

She stiffened when she heard the familiar voice speak her name. She didn't turn toward the sound, for it surely must be her desperate imagination playing tricks upon her.

"Please look at me, Ella."

Ella slowly turned her head toward the voice, so fearful she was mistaken. But it was him. Gabriel. He'd returned, and now stood before her with the same lost look on his face she had put there days ago.

"Gabriel, I—" Her voice was soft and full of regret.

He knelt down on the ground before her and took her hand in his. "Wait. Please let me talk. I've thought about what happened between us at the store, and Ella, I have to tell you, I was so wrong."

She tried to interrupt him but he rushed on.

"After what you said about me leaving you at the end of summer, I realized I needed to either make a commitment or walk away. I couldn't have it both ways. I was falling in love with you, but it scared the hell out of me. After what happened with Sonia I didn't think I could go through something like that again. I needed time to think. After I got home all I could think about was you. I know now what it is I need."

He paused for a moment and reached into his pocket to pull out a small velvet box. Ella gasped when she saw it, and stared at Gabriel in shock as he lifted the lid to reveal a stunning diamond ring.

"I love you, Ella, with all my heart. Without you my life is empty. I cannot bear the thought of spending another day without you, or Calvin. Will you marry me?"

Ella opened her mouth, but no sound would come forth. She swallowed hard, and looked into Gabriel's eyes. "I'm not angry with you. I had just made up my mind to drive into the city tomorrow and track you down. Gabriel, I was wrong, so wrong to say I didn't need you. I do need you. I've been miserable without you."

He got up and took her into his arms. "Please marry me. I love you so much."

"Yes, I'll marry you! I love you too, Gabriel."

~*~

"Do you take this woman to be your bride? Will you love, honor, and cherish her, so long as you both may live?" the minister asked Nicky.

"I will." Nicky's voice was strong and resolute.

Ella stood beside her cousin as her maid of honor, but her eyes were not on the bride and groom. They were on Gabriel, who stood proudly beside Nicky as his best man.

After talking late into the night, Gabriel had finally left for the motel room he'd rented, while Ella practically floated off to bed. Her dreams had been peaceful and full of promise. The next morning, she had shown off her beautiful ring to her family, after first taking Calvin quietly aside to tell him the news. To her relief, Calvin had been overjoyed as he declared he and Darius would be brothers. When Nicky had arrived to join them for breakfast, he had been delighted with the news. Gabriel came by later that morning, and Nicky asked him to stand up for him as his best man at the wedding. He revealed he was going to ask him earlier, but when he'd arrived in town, Gabriel was gone. Nicky said he hadn't asked anyone else because he knew deep down Gabriel would return. Gabriel had accepted the honor only on condition that Nicky return the favor in the spring at his and Ella's wedding.

Ella turned her attention back to the happy couple when the minister told Nicky he may kiss his bride. As the young couple strode happily down the aisle to greet the crowd, Gabriel took Ella's hand in his and they followed them out of the church and toward their own future.

Calvin watched the pair with a happy smile of his own. He tapped his little watch and announced, "It's about time!"

About the Author

Julie is a long time resident of Hamilton, Ontario, where she lives with her husband of 25 years. She has two grown sons who recently left the nest. Working in a library for several years inspired her to pursue her long time love of writing. Please check out her website http://julieparker.yolasite.com/

CPSIA information can be obtained
at www.ICGtesting.com
Printed in the USA
LVHW03s0531240718
584707LV00001B/23/P